GW01179287

This Autograph Edition, printed on Old Stratford paper, is limited to five hundred and four copies, of which this is

No. 157

THE WORKS OF

HENRY VAN DYKE

AVALON EDITION

VOLUME X

❦

POEMS

II

Henry van Dyke
From a bust by William Ordway Partridge

POEMS

BY

HENRY VAN DYKE

VOLUME TWO

NEW YORK
CHARLES SCRIBNER'S SONS
1920

To

JOHN HUSTON FINLEY

CONTENTS

PRO PATRIA

CONTENTS

THE RED FLOWER AND GOLDEN STARS

CONTENTS

IN PRAISE OF POETS

MUSIC

CONTENTS

THE HOUSE OF RIMMON

A DRAMA IN FOUR ACTS

APPENDIX

CARMINA FESTIVA

PRO PATRIA

PATRIA

I WOULD not even ask my heart to say
If I could love another land as well
As thee, my country, had I felt the spell
Of Italy at birth, or learned to obey
The charm of France, or England's mighty sway.
I would not be so much an infidel
As once to dream, or fashion words to tell,
What land could hold my heart from thee away.

For like a law of nature in my blood,
America, I feel thy sovereignty,
And woven through my soul thy vital sign.
My life is but a wave and thou the flood;
I am a leaf and thou the mother-tree;
Nor should I be at all, were I not thine.

June, 1904.

AMERICA

I love thine inland seas,
Thy groves of giant trees,
  Thy rolling plains;
Thy rivers' mighty sweep,
Thy mystic canyons deep,
Thy mountains wild and steep,
  All thy domains;

Thy silver Eastern strands,
Thy Golden Gate that stands
  Wide to the West;
Thy flowery Southland fair,
Thy sweet and crystal air,—
O land beyond compare,
  Thee I love best!

March, 1906.

THE ANCESTRAL DWELLINGS

DEAR to my heart are the ancestral dwellings of America,
Dearer than if they were haunted by ghosts of royal splendour;
They are simple enough to be great in their friendly dignity,—
Homes that were built by the brave beginners of a nation.

I love the old white farmhouses nestled in New England valleys,
Ample and long and low, with elm-trees feathering over them:
Borders of box in the yard, and lilacs, and old-fashioned roses,
A fan-light above the door, and little square panes in the windows,
The wood-shed piled with maple and birch and hickory ready for winter,
The gambrel-roof with its garret crowded with household relics,—
All the tokens of prudent thrift and the spirit of self-reliance.

I love the weather-beaten, shingled houses that front the ocean;
They seem to grow out of the rocks, there is something indomitable about them:

PRO PATRIA

Their backs are bowed, and their sides are covered with
lichens;
Soft in their colour as gray pearls, they are full of a
patient courage.
Facing the briny wind on a lonely shore they stand
undaunted,
While the thin blue pennant of smoke from the square-built chimney
Tells of a haven for man, with room for a hearth and a
cradle.

I love the stately southern mansions with their tall white
columns,
They look through avenues of trees, over fields where
the cotton is growing;
I can see the flutter of white frocks along their shady
porches,
Music and laughter float from the windows, the yards
are full of hounds and horses.
Long since the riders have ridden away, yet the houses
have not forgotten,
They are proud of their name and place, and their doors
are always open,
For the thing they remember best is the pride of their
ancient hospitality.

THE ANCESTRAL DWELLINGS

In the towns I love the discreet and tranquil Quaker
dwellings,
With their demure brick faces and immaculate marble
doorsteps;
And the gabled houses of the Dutch, with their high
stoops and iron railings,
(I can see their little brass knobs shining in the morning
sunlight);
And the solid self-contained houses of the descendants of
the Puritans,
Frowning on the street with their narrow doors and
dormer-windows;
And the triple-galleried, many-pillared mansions of
Charleston,
Standing open sideways in their gardens of roses and
magnolias.

Yes, they are all dear to my heart, and in my eyes they
are beautiful;
For under their roofs were nourished the thoughts that
have made the nation;
The glory and strength of America come from her ancestral dwellings.

July, 1909.

HUDSON'S LAST VOYAGE

THE SHALLOP ON HUDSON BAY

June 22, 1611

ONE sail in sight upon the lonely sea,
And only one! For never ship but mine
Has dared these waters. We were first,
My men, to battle in between the bergs
And floes to these wide waves. This gulf is mine;
I name it! and that flying sail is mine!
And there, hull-down below that flying sail,
The ship that staggers home is mine, mine, mine!
My ship *Discoverie!*

The sullen dogs
Of mutineers, the bitches' whelps that snatched
Their food and bit the hand that nourished them,
Have stolen her. You ingrate Henry Greene,
I picked you from the gutter of Houndsditch,
And paid your debts, and kept you in my house,
And brought you here to make a man of you!
You Robert Juet, ancient, crafty man,
Toothless and tremulous, how many times
Have I employed you as a master's mate
To give you bread? And you Abacuck Prickett,
You sailor-clerk, you salted puritan,
You knew the plot and silently agreed,
Salving your conscience with a pious lie!

HUDSON'S LAST VOYAGE

Yes, all of you—hounds, rebels, thieves! Bring back
My ship!

Too late,—I rave,—they cannot hear
My voice: and if they heard, a drunken laugh
Would be their answer; for their minds have caught
The fatal firmness of the fool's resolve,
That looks like courage but is only fear.
They'll blunder on, and lose my ship, and drown;
Or blunder home to England and be hanged.
Their skeletons will rattle in the chains
Of some tall gibbet on the Channel cliffs,
While passing mariners look up and say:
"Those are the rotten bones of Hudson's men
"Who left their captain in the frozen North!"

O God of justice, why hast Thou ordained
Plans of the wise and actions of the brave
Dependent on the aid of fools and cowards?

Look,—there she goes,—her topsails in the sun
Gleam from the ragged ocean edge, and drop
Clean out of sight! So let the traitors go
Clean out of mind! We'll think of braver things!
Come closer in the boat, my friends. John King,
You take the tiller, keep her head nor'west.
You Philip Staffe, the only one who chose
Freely to share our little shallop's fate,
Rather than travel in the hell-bound ship,—

PRO PATRIA

Too good an English sailor to desert
Your crippled comrades,—try to make them rest
More easy on the thwarts. And John, my son,
My little shipmate, come and lean your head
Against my knee. Do you remember still
The April morn in Ethelburga's church,
Five years ago, when side by side we kneeled
To take the sacrament with all our men,
Before the *Hopewell* left St. Catherine's docks
On our first voyage? It was then I vowed
My sailor-soul and yours to search the sea
Until we found the water-path that leads
From Europe into Asia.

I believe
That God has poured the ocean round His world,
Not to divide, but to unite the lands.
And all the English captains that have dared
In little ships to plough uncharted waves,—
Davis and Drake, Hawkins and Frobisher,
Raleigh and Gilbert,—all the other names,—
Are written in the chivalry of God
As men who served His purpose. I would claim
A place among that knighthood of the sea;
And I have earned it, though my quest should fail!
For, mark me well, the honour of our life
Derives from this: to have a certain aim
Before us always, which our will must seek
Amid the peril of uncertain ways.

Then, though we miss the goal, our search is crowned
With courage, and we find along our path
A rich reward of unexpected things.
Press towards the aim: take fortune as it fares!

I know not why, but something in my heart
Has always whispered, "Westward seek your goal!"
Three times they sent me east, but still I turned
The bowsprit west, and felt among the floes
Of ruttling ice along the Greenland coast,
And down the rugged shore of Newfoundland,
And past the rocky capes and wooded bays
Where Gosnold sailed,—like one who feels his way
With outstretched hand across a darkened room,—
I groped among the inlets and the isles,
To find the passage to the Land of Spice.
I have not found it yet,—but I have found
Things worth the finding!

Son, have you forgot
Those mellow autumn days, two years ago,
When first we sent our little ship *Half-Moon*,—
The flag of Holland floating at her peak,—
Across a sandy bar, and sounded in
Among the channels, to a goodly bay
Where all the navies of the world could ride?
A fertile island that the redmen called
Manhattan, lay above the bay: the land
Around was bountiful and friendly fair.

PRO PATRIA

But never land was fair enough to hold
The seaman from the calling of the sea.
And so we bore to westward of the isle,
Along a mighty inlet, where the tide
Was troubled by a downward-flowing flood
That seemed to come from far away,—perhaps
From some mysterious gulf of Tartary?
Inland we held our course; by palisades
Of naked rock; by rolling hills adorned
With forests rich in timber for great ships;
Through narrows where the mountains shut us in
With frowning cliffs that seemed to bar the stream;
And then through open reaches where the banks
Sloped to the water gently, with their fields
Of corn and lentils smiling in the sun.
Ten days we voyaged through that placid land,
Until we came to shoals, and sent a boat
Upstream to find,—what I already knew,—
We travelled on a river, not a strait.

But what a river! God has never poured
A stream more royal through a land more rich.
Even now I see it flowing in my dream,
While coming ages people it with men
Of manhood equal to the river's pride.
I see the wigwams of the redmen changed
To ample houses, and the tiny plots
Of maize and green tobacco broadened out

To prosperous farms, that spread o'er hill and dale
The many-coloured mantle of their crops.
I see the terraced vineyard on the slope
Where now the fox-grape loops its tangled vine,
And cattle feeding where the red deer roam,
And wild-bees gathered into busy hives
To store the silver comb with golden sweet;
And all the promised land begins to flow
With milk and honey. Stately manors rise
Along the banks, and castles top the hills,
And little villages grow populous with trade,
Until the river runs as proudly as the Rhine,—
The thread that links a hundred towns and towers!
Now looking deeper in my dream, I see
A mighty city covering the isle
They call Manhattan, equal in her state
To all the older capitals of earth,—
The gateway city of a golden world,—
A city girt with masts, and crowned with spires,
And swarming with a million busy men,
While to her open door across the bay
The ships of all the nations flock like doves.
My name will be remembered there, the world
Will say, "This river and this isle were found
By Henry Hudson, on his way to seek
The Northwest Passage."

Yes, I seek it still,—
My great adventure and my guiding star!

PRO PATRIA

For look ye, friends, our voyage is not done;
We hold by hope as long as life endures!
Somewhere among these floating fields of ice,
Somewhere along this westward widening bay,
Somewhere beneath this luminous northern night,
The channel opens to the Farthest East,—
I know it,—and some day a little ship
Will push her bowsprit in, and battle through!
And why not ours,—to-morrow,—who can tell?
The lucky chance awaits the fearless heart!
These are the longest days of all the year;
The world is round and God is everywhere,
And while our shallop floats we still can steer.

So point her up, John King, nor'west by north
We'll keep the honour of a certain aim
Amid the peril of uncertain ways,
And sail ahead, and leave the rest to God.

July, 1909.

SEA-GULLS OF MANHATTAN

Children of the elemental mother,
  Born upon some lonely island shore
Where the wrinkled ripples run and whisper,
  Where the crested billows plunge and roar;
Long-winged, tireless roamers and adventurers,
  Fearless breasters of the wind and sea,
In the far-off solitary places
  I have seen you floating wild and free!

Here the high-built cities rise around you;
  Here the cliffs that tower east and west,
Honeycombed with human habitations,
  Have no hiding for the sea-bird's nest:
Here the river flows begrimed and troubled;
  Here the hurrying, panting vessels fume,
Restless, up and down the watery highway,
  While a thousand chimneys vomit gloom.

Toil and tumult, conflict and confusion,
  Clank and clamour of the vast machine
Human hands have built for human bondage—
  Yet amid it all you float serene;
Circling, soaring, sailing, swooping lightly
  Down to glean your harvest from the wave;
In your heritage of air and water,
  You have kept the freedom Nature gave.

PRO PATRIA

Even so the wild-woods of Manhattan
  Saw your wheeling flocks of white and gray;
Even so you fluttered, followed, floated,
  Round the *Half-Moon* creeping up the bay;
Even so your voices creaked and chattered,
  Laughing shrilly o'er the tidal rips,
While your black and beady eyes were glistening
  Round the sullen British prison-ships.

Children of the elemental mother,
  Fearless floaters 'mid the double blue,
From the crowded boats that cross the ferries
  Many a longing heart goes out to you.
Though the cities climb and close around us,
  Something tells us that our souls are free,
While the sea-gulls fly above the harbour,
  While the river flows to meet the sea!

December, 1905.

A BALLAD OF CLAREMONT HILL

THE roar of the city is low,
Muffled by new-fallen snow,
And the sign of the wintry moon is small and round and still.
Will you come with me to-night,
To see a pleasant sight
Away on the river-side, at the edge of Claremont Hill?

"And what shall we see there,
But streets that are new and bare,
And many a desolate place that the city is coming to fill;
And a soldier's tomb of stone,
And a few trees standing alone—
Will you walk for that through the cold, to the edge of Claremont Hill?"

But there's more than that for me,
In the place that I fain would see:
There's a glimpse of the grace that helps us all to bear life's ill,
A touch of the vital breath
That keeps the world from death,
A flower that never fades, on the edge of Claremont Hill.

For just where the road swings round,
In a narrow strip of ground,

PRO PATRIA

Where a group of forest trees are lingering fondly still,
There's a grave of the olden time,
When the garden bloomed in its prime,
And the children laughed and sang on the edge of Claremont Hill.

The marble is pure and white,
And even in this dim light,
You may read the simple words that are written there if you will;
You may hear a father tell
Of the child he loved so well,
A hundred years ago, on the edge of Claremont Hill.

The tide of the city has rolled
Across that bower of old,
And blotted out the beds of the rose and the daffodil;
But the little playmate sleeps,
And the shrine of love still keeps
A record of happy days, on the edge of Claremont Hill.

The river is pouring down
To the crowded, careless town,
Where the intricate wheels of trade are grinding on like a mill;
But the clamorous noise and strife
Of the hurrying waves of life
Flow soft by this haven of peace on the edge of Claremont Hill.

A BALLAD OF CLAREMONT HILL

And after all, my friend,
When the tale of our years shall end,
Be it long or short, or lowly or great, as God may will,
What better praise could we hear,
Than this of the child so dear:
You have made my life more sweet, on the edge of Claremont Hill?

December, 1896.

URBS CORONATA

(Song for the City College of New York)

O YOUNGEST of the giant brood
  Of cities far-renowned;
In wealth and glory thou hast passed
  Thy rivals at a bound;
Thou art a mighty queen, New York;
  And how wilt thou be crowned?

"Weave me no palace-wreath of Pride,"
  The royal city said;
"Nor forge of frowning fortress-walls
  A helmet for my head;
But let me wear a diadem
  Of Wisdom's towers instead."

She bowed herself, she spent herself,
  She wrought her will forsooth,
And set upon her island height
  A citadel of Truth,
A house of Light, a home of Thought,
  A shrine of noble Youth.

URBS CORONATA

Stand here, ye City College towers,
  And look both up and down;
Remember all who wrought for you
  Within the toiling town;
Remember all their hopes for you,
  And *be* the City's Crown.

June, 1908.

MERCY FOR ARMENIA

I

THE TURK'S WAY

STAND back, ye messengers of mercy! Stand
Far off, for I will save my troubled folk
In my own way. So the false Sultan spoke;
And Europe, hearkening to his base command,
Stood still to see him heal his wounded land.
Through blinding snows of winter and through smoke
Of burning towns, she saw him deal the stroke
Of cruel mercy that his hate had planned.
Unto the prisoners and the sick he gave
New tortures, horrible, without a name;
Unto the thirsty, blood to drink; a sword
Unto the hungry; with a robe of shame
He clad the naked, making life abhorred;
He saved by slaughter, and denied a grave.

II

AMERICA'S WAY

But thou, my country, though no fault be thine
For that red horror far across the sea;
Though not a tortured wretch can point to thee,
And curse thee for the selfishness supine
Of those great Powers that cowardly combine

MERCY FOR ARMENIA

To shield the Turk in his iniquity;
Yet, since thy hand is innocent and free,
Arise, and show the world the way divine!
Thou canst not break the oppressor's iron rod,
But thou canst help and comfort the oppressed;
Thou canst not loose the captive's heavy chain,
But thou canst bind his wounds and soothe his pain.
Armenia calls thee, Sovereign of the West,
To play the Good Samaritan for God.

1896.

SICILY, DECEMBER, 1908

O GARDEN isle, beloved by Sun and Sea,
  Whose bluest billows kiss thy curving bays,
  Whose light infolds thy hills with golden rays,
Filling with fruit each dark-leaved orange-tree,
What hidden hatred hath the Earth for thee,
  That once again, in these dark, dreadful days,
  Breaks forth in trembling rage, and swiftly lays
Thy beauty waste in wreck and agony!
Is Nature, then, a strife of jealous powers,
  And man the plaything of unconscious fate?
    Not so, my troubled heart! God reigns above,
And man is greatest in his darkest hours.
  Walking amid the cities desolate,
    Behold the Son of God in human love!

Tertius and Henry van Dyke.

"COME BACK AGAIN, JEANNE D'ARC"

THE land was broken in despair,
The princes quarrelled in the dark,
When clear and tranquil, through the troubled air
Of selfish minds and wills that did not dare,
Your star arose, Jeanne d'Arc.

O virgin breast with lilies white,
O sun-burned hand that bore the lance,
You taught the prayer that helps men to unite,
You brought the courage equal to the fight,
You gave a heart to France!

Your king was crowned, your country free,
At Rheims you had your soul's desire:
And then, at Rouen, maid of Domrémy,
The black-robed judges gave your victory
The martyr's crown of fire.

And now again the times are ill,
And doubtful leaders miss the mark;
The people lack the single faith and will
To make them one,—your country needs you still,—
Come back again, Jeanne d'Arc!

PRO PATRIA

O woman-star, arise once more
  And shine to bid your land advance:
The old heroic trust in God restore,
Renew the brave, unselfish hopes of yore,
      And give a heart to France!

Paris, July, 1909.

NATIONAL MONUMENTS

COUNT not the cost of honour to the dead!
The tribute that a mighty nation pays
To those who loved her well in former days
Means more than gratitude for glories fled;
For every noble man that she hath bred,
Lives in the bronze and marble that we raise,
Immortalised by art's immortal praise,
To lead our sons as he our fathers led.

These monuments of manhood strong and high
Do more than forts or battle-ships to keep
Our dear-bought liberty. They fortify
The heart of youth with valour wise and deep;
They build eternal bulwarks, and command
Immortal hosts to guard our native land.

February, 1905.

THE MONUMENT OF FRANCIS MAKEMIE

(Presbyter of Christ in America, 1683–1708)

To thee, plain hero of a rugged race,
  We bring the meed of praise too long delayed!
  Thy fearless word and faithful work have made
For God's Republic firmer resting-place
In this New World: for thou hast preached the grace
  And power of Christ in many a forest glade,
  Teaching the truth that leaves men unafraid
Of frowning tyranny or death's dark face.

Oh, who can tell how much we owe to thee,
  Makemie, and to labour such as thine,
  For all that makes America the shrine
Of faith untrammelled and of conscience free?
Stand here, gray stone, and consecrate the sod
Where rests this brave Scotch-Irish man of God!

April, 1908.

THE STATUE OF SHERMAN BY ST. GAUDENS

This is the soldier brave enough to tell
The glory-dazzled world that 'war is hell':
Lover of peace, he looks beyond the strife,
And rides through hell to save his country's life.

April, 1904.

"AMERICA FOR ME"

'Tis fine to see the Old World, and travel up and down
Among the famous palaces and cities of renown,
To admire the crumbly castles and the statues of the
kings,—
But now I think I've had enough of antiquated things.

So it's home again, and home again, America for me!
My heart is turning home again, and there I long to be,
In the land of youth and freedom beyond the ocean bars,
Where the air is full of sunlight and the flag is full of stars.

Oh, London is a man's town, there's power in the air;
And Paris is a woman's town, with flowers in her hair;
And it's sweet to dream in Venice, and it's great to study
Rome;
But when it comes to living there is no place like home.

I like the German fir-woods, in green battalions drilled;
I like the gardens of Versailles with flashing fountains
filled;
But, oh, to take your hand, my dear, and ramble for a
day
In the friendly western woodland where Nature has her
way!

"AMERICA FOR ME"

I know that Europe's wonderful, yet something seems to
lack:
The Past is too much with her, and the people looking
back.
But the glory of the Present is to make the Future free,—
We love our land for what she is and what she is to be.

Oh, it's home again, and home again, America for me!
I want a ship that's westward bound to plough the rolling
sea,
To the blessèd Land of Room Enough beyond the ocean
bars,
Where the air is full of sunlight and the flag is full of stars.

June, 1909.

THE BUILDERS

ODE FOR THE HUNDRED AND FIFTIETH ANNIVERSARY OF PRINCETON COLLEGE

October 21, 1896

I

INTO the dust of the making of man
Spirit was breathed when his life began,
Lifting him up from his low estate,
With masterful passion, the wish to create.
Out of the dust of his making, man
Fashioned his works as the ages ran;
Fortress, and palace, and temple, and tower,
Filling the world with the proof of his power.
Over the dust that awaits him, man,
Building the walls that his pride doth plan,
Dreams they will stand in the light of the sun
Bearing his name till Time is done.

II

The monuments of mortals
  Are as the glory of the grass;
Through Time's dim portals
  A voiceless, viewless wind doth pass,
The blossoms fall before it in a day,

The forest monarchs year by year decay,
And man's great buildings slowly fade away.
One after one,
They pay to that dumb breath
The tribute of their death,
And are undone.
The towers incline to dust,
The massive girders rust,
The domes dissolve in air,
The pillars that upbear
The lofty arches crumble, stone by stone,
While man the builder looks about him in despair,
For all his works of pride and power are overthrown.

III

A Voice came from the sky:
"Set thy desires more high.
Thy buildings fade away
Because thou buildest clay.
Now make the fabric sure
With stones that will endure!
Hewn from the spiritual rock,
The immortal towers of the soul
At Death's dissolving touch shall mock,
And stand secure while æons roll."

PRO PATRIA

IV

Well did the wise in heart rejoice
To hear the summons of that Voice,
And patiently begin
The builder's work within,
Houses not made with hands,
Nor founded on the sands.
And thou, Reverèd Mother, at whose call
We come to keep thy joyous festival,
And celebrate thy labours on the walls of Truth
Through sevenscore years and ten of thine eternal youth—
A master builder thou,
And on thy shining brow,
Like Cybele, in fadeless light dost wear
A diadem of turrets strong and fair.

V

I see thee standing in a lonely land,
But late and hardly won from solitude,
Unpopulous and rude,—
On that far western shore I see thee stand,
Like some young goddess from a brighter strand,
While in thine eyes a radiant thought is born,
Enkindling all thy beauty like the morn.
Sea-like the forest rolled, in waves of green,
And few the lights that glimmered, leagues between.

THE BUILDERS

High in the north, for fourscore years alone
Fair Harvard's earliest beacon-tower had shone
When Yale was lighted, and an answering ray
Flashed from the meadows by New Haven Bay.
But deeper spread the forest, and more dark,
Where first Neshaminy received the spark
Of sacred learning to a woodland camp,
And Old Log College glowed with Tennant's lamp.
Thine, Alma Mater, was the larger sight,
That saw the future of that trembling light,
And thine the courage, thine the stronger will,
That built its loftier home on Princeton Hill.

"New light!" men cried, and murmured that it came
From an unsanctioned source with lawless flame;
It shone too free, for still the church and school
Must only shine according to their rule.
But Princeton answered, in her nobler mood,
"God made the light, and all the light is good.
There is no war between the old and new;
The conflict lies between the false and true.
The stars, that high in heaven their courses run,
In glory differ, but their light is one.
The beacons, gleaming o'er the sea of life,
Are rivals but in radiance, not in strife.
Shine on, ye sister-towers, across the night!
I too will build a lasting house of light."

VI

Brave was that word of faith and bravely was it kept;
With never-wearying zeal that faltered not, nor slept,
Our Alma Mater toiled, and while she firmly laid
The deep foundation-walls, at all her toil she prayed.
And men who loved the truth because it made them free,
And clearly saw the twofold Word of God agree,
Reading from Nature's book and from the Bible's page
By the same inward ray that grows from age to age,
Were built like living stones that beacon to uplift,
And drawing light from heaven gave to the world the gift.
Nor ever, while they searched the secrets of the earth,
Or traced the stream of life through mystery to its birth,
Nor ever, while they taught the lightning-flash to bear
The messages of man in silence through the air,
Fell from their home of light one false, perfidious ray
To blind the trusting heart, or lead the life astray.
But still, while knowledge grew more luminous and broad
It lit the path of faith and showed the way to God.

VII

Yet not for peace alone
  Labour the builders.
Work that in peace has grown
Swiftly is overthrown,
When in the darkening skies

Storm-clouds of wrath arise,
And through the cannon's crash,
War's deadly lightning-flash
  Smites and bewilders.
Ramparts of strength must frown
Round every placid town
  And city splendid;
All that our fathers wrought
With true prophetic thought,
  Must be defended!

VIII

But who could raise protecting walls for thee,
Thou young, defenceless land of liberty?
Or who could build a fortress strong enough,
Or stretch a mighty bulwark long enough
    To hold thy far-extended coast
    Against the overweening host
That took the open path across the sea,
      And like a tempest poured
      Their desolating horde,
To quench thy dawning light in gloom of tyranny?
Yet not unguarded thou wert found
When on thy shore with sullen sound
The blaring trumpets of an unjust king
Proclaimed invasion. From the ground,
In freedom's darkest hour, there seemed to spring

Unconquerable walls for her defence;
Not trembling, like those battlements of stone
That fell when Joshua's horns were blown;
But firm and stark the living rampart rose,
To meet the onset of imperious foes
With a long line of brave, unyielding men.
This was thy fortress, well-defended land,
And on these walls, the patient, building hand
Of Princeton laboured with the force of ten.
Her sons were foremost in the furious fight;
Her sons were firmest to uphold the right
In council-chambers of the new-born State,
And prove that he who would be free must first be great
In heart, and high in thought, and strong
In purpose not to do or suffer wrong.
Such were the men, impregnable to fear,
Whose souls were framed and fashioned here;
And when war shook the land with threatening shock,
The men of Princeton stood like muniments of rock.
Nor has the breath of Time
Dissolved that proud array
Of never-broken strength:
For though the rocks decay,
And all the iron bands
Of earthly strongholds are unloosed at length,
And buried deep in gray oblivion's sands;
The work that heroes' hands
Wrought in the light of freedom's natal day

Shall never fade away,
But lifts itself, sublime
Into a lucid sphere,
For ever calm and clear,
Preserving in the memory of the fathers' deed,
A never-failing fortress for their children's need.
There we confirm our hearts to-day, and read
On many a stone the signature of fame,
The builder's mark, our Alma Mater's name.

IX

Bear with us then a moment, while we turn
From all the present splendours of this place—
The lofty towers that like a dream have grown
Where once old Nassau Hall stood all alone—
Back to that ancient time, with hearts that burn
In filial gratitude, to trace
The glory of our mother's best degree,
In that "high son of Liberty,"
Who like a granite block,
Riven from Scotland's rock,
Stood loyal here to keep Columbia free.
Born far away beyond the ocean's tide,
He found his fatherland upon this side;
And every drop of ardent blood that ran
Through his great heart, was true American.
He held no fealty to a distant throne,

But made his new-found country's cause his own.
In peril and distress,
In toil and weariness,
When darkness overcast her
With shadows of disaster,
And voices of confusion
Proclaimed her hope delusion,
Robed in his preacher's gown,
He dared the danger down;
Like some old prophet chanting an inspired rune
In freedom's councils rang the voice of Witherspoon.

And thou, my country, write it on thy heart:
Thy sons are they who nobly take thy part;
Who dedicates his manhood at thy shrine,
Wherever born, is born a son of thine.
Foreign in name, but not in soul, they come
To find in thee their long-desired home;
Lovers of liberty and haters of disorder,
They shall be built in strength along thy border.

Dream not thy future foes
Will all be foreign-born!
Turn thy clear look of scorn
Upon thy children who oppose
Their passions wild and policies of shame
To wreck the righteous splendour of thy name.
Untaught and overconfident they rise,

THE BUILDERS

With folly on their lips, and envy in their eyes:
Strong to destroy, but powerless to create,
And ignorant of all that made our fathers great,
Their hands would take away thy golden crown,
And shake the pillars of thy freedom down
In Anarchy's ocean, dark and desolate.
  O should that storm descend,
  What fortress shall defend
  The land our fathers wrought for,
  The liberties they fought for?
  What bulwark shall secure
Her shrines of law, and keep her founts of justice pure?
      Then, ah then,
    As in the olden days,
  The builders must upraise
  A rampart of indomitable men.
      And once again,
Dear Mother, if thy heart and hand be true,
There will be building work for thee to do;
  Yea, more than once again,
  Thou shalt win lasting praise,
And never-dying honour shall be thine,
For setting many stones in that illustrious line,
To stand unshaken in the swirling strife,
And guard their country's honour as her life.

PRO PATRIA

X

Softly, my harp, and let me lay the touch
Of silence on these rudely clanging strings;
    For he who sings
Even of noble conflicts overmuch,
Loses the inward sense of better things;
  And he who makes a boast
Of knowledge, darkens that which counts the most,—
  The insight of a wise humility
That reverently adores what none can see.
  The glory of our life below
Comes not from what we do, or what we know,
    But dwells forevermore in what we are.
    There is an architecture grander far
      Than all the fortresses of war,
      More inextinguishably bright
    Than learning's lonely towers of light.
    Framing its walls of faith and hope and love
      In souls of men, it lifts above
      The frailty of our earthly home
        An everlasting dome;
    The sanctuary of the human host,
    The living temple of the Holy Ghost.

THE BUILDERS

XI

If music led the builders long ago,
When Arthur planned the halls of Camelot,
And made the royal city grow,
Fair as a flower in that forsaken spot;
What sweeter music shall we bring,
To weave a harmony divine
Of prayer and holy thought
Into the labours of this loftier shrine,
This consecrated hill,
Where through so many a year
Our Alma Mater's hand hath wrought,
With toil serene and still,
And heavenly hope, to rear
Eternal dwellings for the Only King?
Here let no martial trumpets blow,
Nor instruments of pride proclaim
The loud exultant notes of fame!
But let the chords be clear and low,
And let the anthem deeper grow,
And let it move more solemnly and slow;
For only such an ode
Can seal the harmony
Of that deep masonry
Wherein the soul of man is framed for God's abode.

PRO PATRIA

XII

O Thou whose boundless love bestows
  The joy of earth, the hope of Heaven,
And whose unchartered mercy flows
  O'er all the blessings Thou hast given;
Thou by whose light alone we see;
And by whose truth our souls set free
Are made imperishably strong;
Hear Thou the solemn music of our song.

Grant us the knowledge that we need
  To solve the questions of the mind,
And light our candle while we read,
  To keep our hearts from going blind;
Enlarge our vision to behold
The wonders Thou hast wrought of old;
Reveal thyself in every law,
And gild the towers of truth with holy awe.

Be Thou our strength if war's wild gust
  Shall rage around us, loud and fierce;
Confirm our souls and let our trust
  Be like a shield that none can pierce;
Renew the courage that prevails,
The steady faith that never fails,
And make us stand in every fight
Firm as a fortress to defend the right.

THE BUILDERS

O God, control us as Thou wilt,
  And guide the labour of our hand;
Let all our work be surely built
  As Thou, the architect, hast planned;
But whatso'er thy power shall make
Of these frail lives, do not forsake
Thy dwelling: let thy presence rest
For ever in the temple of our breast.

SPIRIT OF THE EVERLASTING BOY

ODE FOR THE HUNDREDTH ANNIVERSARY OF LAWRENCEVILLE SCHOOL

June 11, 1910

I

THE British bard who looked on Eton's walls,
Endeared by distance in the pearly gray
And soft aerial blue that ever falls
On English landscape with the dying day,
Beheld in thought his boyhood far away,
Its random raptures and its festivals
    Of noisy mirth,
The brief illusion of its idle joys,
And mourned that none of these can stay
With men, whom life inexorably calls
To face the grim realities of earth.
His pensive fancy pictured there at play
From year to year the careless bands of boys,
Unconscious victims kept in golden state,
    While haply they await
The dark approach of disenchanting Fate,
    To hale them to the sacrifice
Of Pain and Penury and Grief and Care,
Slow-withering Age, or Failure's swift despair.
Half-pity and half-envy dimmed the eyes

Of that old poet, gazing on the scene
Where long ago his youth had flowed serene,
And all the burden of his ode was this:
"Where ignorance is bliss,
'Tis folly to be wise."

II

But not for us, O plaintive elegist,
Thine epicedial tone of sad farewell
To joy in wisdom and to thought in youth!
Our western Muse would keep her tryst
With sunrise, not with sunset, and foretell
In boyhood's bliss the dawn of manhood's truth.

III

O spirit of the everlasting boy,
Alert, elate,
And confident that life is good,
Thou knockest boldly at the gate,
In hopeful hardihood,
Eager to enter and enjoy
Thy new estate.

Through the old house thou runnest everywhere,
Bringing a breath of folly and fresh air.
Ready to make a treasure of each toy,
Or break them all in discontented mood;

PRO PATRIA

Fearless of Fate,
Yet strangely fearful of a comrade's laugh;
Reckless and timid, hard and sensitive;
In talk a rebel, full of mocking chaff,
At heart devout conservative;
In love with love, yet hating to be kissed;
Inveterate optimist,
And judge severe,
In reason cloudy but in feeling clear;
Keen critic, ardent hero-worshipper,
Impatient of restraint in little ways,
Yet ever ready to confer
On chosen leaders boundless power and praise;
Adventurous spirit burning to explore
Untrodden paths where hidden danger lies,
And homesick heart looking with wistful eyes
Through every twilight to a mother's door;
Thou daring, darling, inconsistent boy,
How dull the world would be
Without thy presence, dear barbarian,
And happy lord of high futurity!
Be what thou art, our trouble and our joy,
Our hardest problem and our brightest hope!
And while thine elders lead thee up the slope
Of knowledge, let them learn from teaching thee
That vital joy is part of nature's plan,
And he who keeps the spirit of the boy
Shall gladly grow to be a happy man.

SPIRIT OF THE EVERLASTING BOY

IV

What constitutes a school?
Not ancient halls and ivy-mantled towers,
Where dull traditions rule
With heavy hand youth's lightly springing powers;
Not spacious pleasure courts,
And lofty temples of athletic fame,
Where devotees of sports
Mistake a pastime for life's highest aim;
Not fashion, nor renown
Of wealthy patronage and rich estate;
No, none of these can crown
A school with light and make it truly great.
But masters, strong and wise,
Who teach because they love the teacher's task,
And find their richest prize
In eyes that open and in minds that ask;
And boys, with heart aglow
To try their youthful vigour on their work,
Eager to learn and grow,
And quick to hate a coward or a shirk:
These constitute a school,—
A vital forge of weapons keen and bright,
Where living sword and tool
Are tempered for true toil or noble fight!
But let not wisdom scorn
The hours of pleasure in the playing fields:

There also strength is born,
And every manly game a virtue yields.
Fairness and self-control,
Good-humour, pluck, and patience in the race,
Will make a lad heart-whole
To win with honour, lose without disgrace.
Ah, well for him who gains
In such a school apprenticeship to life:
With him the joy of youth remains
In later lessons and in larger strife!

V

On Jersey's rolling plain, where Washington,
In midnight marching at the head
Of ragged regiments, his army led
To Princeton's victory of the rising sun;
Here in this liberal land, by battle won
For Freedom and the rule
Of equal rights for every child of man,
Arose a democratic school,
To train a virile race of sons to bear
With thoughtful joy the name American,
And serve the God who heard their father's prayer.
No cloister, dreaming in a world remote
From that real world wherein alone we live;
No mimic court, where titled names denote
A dignity that only worth can give;

But here a friendly house of learning stood,
With open door beside the broad highway,
And welcomed lads to study and to play
In generous rivalry of brotherhood.
A hundred years have passed, and Lawrenceville,
In beauty and in strength renewed,
Stands with her open portal still,
And neither time nor fortune brings
To her deep spirit any change of mood,
Or faltering from the faith she held of old.
Still to the democratic creed she clings:
That manhood needs nor rank nor gold
To make it noble in our eyes;
That every boy is born with royal right,
From blissful ignorance to rise
To joy more lasting and more bright,
In mastery of body and of mind,
King of himself and servant of mankind.

VI

Old Lawrenceville,
Thy happy bell
Shall ring to-day,
O'er vale and hill,
O'er mead and dell,
While far away,
With silent thrill,

PRO PATRIA

The echoes roll
Through many a soul,
That knew thee well,
In boyhood's day,
And loves thee still.

Ah, who can tell
How far away,
Some sentinel
Of God's good will,
In forest cool,
Or desert gray,
By lonely pool,
Or barren hill,
Shall faintly hear,
With inward ear,
The chiming bell,
Of his old school,
Through darkness pealing;
And lowly kneeling,
Shall feel the spell
Of grateful tears
His eyelids fill;
And softly pray
To Him who hears:
God bless old Lawrenceville!

TEXAS

A DEMOCRATIC ODE *

I

THE WILD-BEES

All along the Brazos river,
All along the Colorado,
In the valleys and the lowlands
Where the trees were tall and stately,
In the rich and rolling meadows
Where the grass was full of wild-flowers,
Came a humming and a buzzing,
Came the murmur of a going
To and fro among the tree-tops,
Far and wide across the meadows.
And the red-men in their tepees
Smoked their pipes of clay and listened.
"What is this?" they asked in wonder;
"Who can give the sound a meaning?
Who can understand the language
Of this going in the tree-tops?"
Then the wisest of the Tejas
Laid his pipe aside and answered:
"O my brothers, these are people,
Very little, winged people,

* Read at the Dedication of the Rice Institute, Houston, Texas, October, 1912.

PRO PATRIA

Countless, busy, banded people,
Coming humming through the timber.
These are tribes of bees, united
By a single aim and purpose,
To possess the Tejas' country,
Gather harvest from the prairies,
Store their wealth among the timber.
These are hive and honey makers,
Sent by Manito to warn us
That the white men now are coming,
With their women and their children.
Not the fiery filibusters
Passing wildly in a moment,
Like a flame across the prairies,
Like a whirlwind through the forest,
Leaving empty lands behind them!
Not the Mexicans and Spaniards,
Indolent and proud hidalgos,
Dwelling in their haciendas,
Dreaming, talking of tomorrow,
While their cattle graze around them,
And their fickle revolutions
Change the rulers, not the people!
Other folk are these who follow
When the wild-bees come to warn us;
These are hive and honey makers,
These are busy, banded people,
Roaming far to swarm and settle,

TEXAS

Working every day for harvest,
Fighting hard for peace and order,
Worshipping as queens their women,
Making homes and building cities
Full of riches and of trouble.
All our hunting-grounds must vanish,
All our lodges fall before them,
All our customs and traditions,
All our happy life of freedom,
Fade away like smoke before them.
Come, my brothers, strike your tepees,
Call your women, load your ponies!
Let us take the trail to westward,
Where the plains are wide and open,
Where the bison-herds are gathered
Waiting for our feathered arrows.
We will live as lived our fathers,
Gleaners of the gifts of nature,
Hunters of the unkept cattle,
Men whose women run to serve them.
If the toiling bees pursue us,
If the white men seek to tame us,
We will fight them off and flee them,
Break their hives and take their honey,
Moving westward, ever westward,
There to live as lived our fathers."
So the red-men drove their ponies,
With the tent-poles trailing after,

PRO PATRIA

Out along the path to sunset,
While along the river valleys
Swarmed the wild-bees, the forerunners;
And the white men, close behind them,
Men of mark from old Missouri,
Men of daring from Kentucky,
Tennessee, Louisiana,
Men of many States and races,
Bringing wives and children with them,
Followed up the wooded valleys,
Spread across the rolling prairies,
Raising homes and reaping harvests.
Rude the toil that tried their patience,
Fierce the fights that proved their courage,
Rough the stone and tough the timber
Out of which they built their order!
Yet they never failed nor faltered,
And the instinct of their swarming
Made them one and kept them working,
Till their toil was crowned with triumph,
And the country of the Tejas
Was the fertile land of Texas.

TEXAS

II

THE LONE STAR

Behold a star appearing in the South,
A star that shines apart from other stars,
    Ruddy and fierce like Mars!
Out of the reeking smoke of cannon's mouth
That veils the slaughter of the Alamo,
    Where heroes face the foe,
One man against a score, with blood-choked breath
Shouting the watchword, "Victory or Death—"
Out of the dreadful cloud that settles low
    On Goliad's plain,
Where thrice a hundred prisoners lie slain
Beneath the broken word of Mexico—
Out of the fog of factions and of feuds
    That ever drifts and broods
Above the bloody path of border war,
    Leaps the Lone Star!

What light is this that does not dread the dark?
What star is this that fights a stormy way
    To San Jacinto's field of victory?
    It is the fiery spark
    That burns within the breast
Of Anglo-Saxon men, who can not rest
    Under a tyrant's sway;
    The upward-leading ray

That guides the brave who give their lives away
    Rather than not be free!
O question not, but honour every name,
Travis and Crockett, Bowie, Bonham, Ward,
Fannin and King, and all who drew the sword
And dared to die for Texan liberty!
Yea, write them all upon the roll of fame,
But no less love and equal honour give
To those who paid the longer sacrifice—
Austin and Houston, Burnet, Rusk, Lamar
And all the stalwart men who dared to live
Long years of service to the lonely star.

Great is the worth of such heroic souls:
Amid the strenuous turmoil of their deeds,
They clearly speak of something that controls
The higher breeds of men by higher needs
Than bees, content with honey in their hives!
    Ah, not enough the narrow lives
  On profitable toil intent!
And not enough the guerdons of success
Garnered in homes of affluent selfishness!
    A noble discontent
    Cries for a wider scope
To use the wider wings of human hope;
    A vision of the common good
Opens the prison-door of solitude;
    And, once beyond the wall,

TEXAS

Breathing the ampler air,
The heart becomes aware
That life without a country is not life at all.
A country worthy of a freeman's love;
A country worthy of a good man's prayer;
A country strong, and just, and brave, and fair,—
A woman's form of beauty throned above
The shrine where noble aspirations meet—
To live for her is great, to die is sweet!

Heirs of the rugged pioneers
Who dreamed this dream and made it true,
Remember that they dreamed for you.
They did not fear their fate
In those tempestuous years,
But put their trust in God, and with keen eyes,
Trained in the open air for looking far,
They saw the many-million-acred land
Won from the desert by their hand,
Swiftly among the nations rise,—
Texas a sovereign State,
And on her brow a star!

PRO PATRIA

III

THE CONSTELLATION

How strange that the nature of light is a thing beyond our ken,
And the flame of the tiniest candle flows from a fountain sealed!
How strange that the meaning of life, in the little lives of men,
So often baffles our search with a mystery unrevealed!

But the larger life of man, as it moves in its secular sweep,
Is the working out of a Sovereign Will whose ways appear;
And the course of the journeying stars on the dark blue boundless deep,
Is the place where our science rests in the reign of law most clear.

I would read the story of Texas as if it were written on high;
I would look from afar to follow her path through the calms and storms;
With a faith in the worldwide sway of the Reason that rules in the sky,
And gathers and guides the starry host in clusters and swarms.

TEXAS

When she rose in the pride of her youth, she seemed to be moving apart,
As a single star in the South, self-limited, self-possessed;
But the law of the constellation was written deep in her heart,
And she heard when her sisters called, from the North and the East and the West.

They were drawn together and moved by a common hope and aim—
The dream of a sign that should rule a third of the heavenly arch;
The soul of a people spoke in their call, and Texas came
To enter the splendid circle of States in their onward march.

So the glory gathered and grew and spread from sea to sea,
And the stars of the great republic lent each other light;
For all were bound together in strength, and each was free—
Suddenly broke the tempest out of the ancient night!

It came as a clash of the force that drives and the force that draws;
And the stars were riven asunder, the heavens were desolate,

PRO PATRIA

While brother fought with brother, each for his country's cause:
But the country of one was the Nation, the country of other the State.

Oh, who shall measure the praise or blame in a strife so vast?
And who shall speak of traitors or tyrants when all were true?
We lift our eyes to the sky, and rejoice that the storm is past,
And we thank the God of all that the Union shines in the blue.

Yea, it glows with the glory of peace and the hope of a mighty race,
High over the grave of broken chains and buried hates;
And the great, big star of Texas is shining clear in its place
In the constellate symbol and sign of the free United States.

TEXAS

IV

AFTER THE PIONEERS

After the pioneers—
Big-hearted, big-handed lords of the axe and the plow
and the rifle,
Tan-faced tamers of horses and lands, themselves remaining tameless,
Full of fighting, labour and romance, lovers of rude adventure—
After the pioneers have cleared the way to their homes
and graves on the prairies:

After the State-builders—
Zealous and jealous men, dreamers, debaters, often at
odds with each other,
All of them sure it is well to toil and to die, if need be,
Just for the sake of founding a country to leave to their
children—
After the builders have done their work and written their
names upon it:

After the civil war—
Wildest of all storms, cruel and dark and seemingly
wasteful,
Tearing up by the root the vines that were splitting the
old foundations,

PRO PATRIA

Washing away with a rain of blood and tears the dust of
slavery,
After the cyclone has passed and the sky is fair to the
far horizon;
After the era of plenty and peace has come with full
hands to Texas,
Then—what then?

Is it to be the life of an indolent heir, fat-witted and self-
contented,
Dwelling at ease in the house that others have builded,
Boasting about the country for which he has done
nothing?
Is it to be an age of corpulent, deadly-dull prosperity,
Richer and richer crops to nourish a race of Philistines,
Bigger and bigger cities full of the same confusion and
sorrow,
The people increasing mightily but no increase of the joy?
Is this what the forerunners wished and toiled to win
for you,
This the reward of war and the fruitage of high en-
deavor,
This the goal of your hopes and the vision that satisfies
you?

Nay, stand up and answer—I can read what is in your
hearts—
You, the children of those who followed the wild-bees,

TEXAS

You, the children of those who served the Lone Star,
Now that the hives are full and the star is fixed in the constellation,
I know that the best of you still are lovers of sweetness and light!

You hunger for honey that comes from invisible gardens;
Pure, translucent, golden thoughts and feelings and inspirations,
Sweetness of all the best that has bloomed in the mind of man.
You rejoice in the light that is breaking along the borders of science;
The hidden rays that enable a man to look through a wall of stone;
The unseen, fire-filled wings that carry his words across the ocean;
The splendid gift of flight that shines, half-captured, above him;
The gleam of a thousand half-guessed secrets, just ready to be discovered!
You dream and devise great things for the coming race—
Children of yours who shall people and rule the domain of Texas;
They shall know, they shall comprehend more than their fathers,
They shall grow in the vigour of well-rounded manhood and womanhood,

PRO PATRIA

Riper minds, richer hearts, finer souls, the only true wealth of a nation—
The league-long fields of the State are pledged to ensure this harvest!

Your old men have dreamed this dream and your young men have seen this vision.
The age of romance has not gone, it is only beginning;
Greater words than the ear of man has heard are waiting to be spoken,
Finer arts than the eyes of man have seen are sleeping to be awakened:
Science exploring the scope of the world,
Poetry breathing the hope of the world,
Music to measure and lead the onward march of man!

Come, ye honoured and welcome guests from the elder nations,
Princes of science and arts and letters,
Look on the walls that embody the generous dream of one of the old men of Texas,
Enter these halls of learning that rise in the land of the pioneer's log-cabin,
Read the confessions of faith that are carved on the stones around you:
Faith in the worth of the smallest fact and the laws that govern the starbeams,

TEXAS

Faith in the beauty of truth and the truth of perfect
beauty,
Faith in the God who creates the souls of men by knowledge and love and worship.

This is the faith of the New Democracy—
Proud and humble, patiently pressing forward,
Praising her heroes of old and training her future leaders,
Seeking her crown in a nobler race of men and women—
After the pioneers, sweetness and light!

October, 1912.

WHO FOLLOW THE FLAG

PHI BETA KAPPA ODE
HARVARD UNIVERSITY

June 30, 1910

I

All day long in the city's canyon-street,
With its populous cliffs alive on either side,
I saw a river of marching men like a tide
Flowing after the flag: and the rhythmic beat
Of the drums, and the bugles' resonant blare
Metred the tramp, tramp, tramp of a myriad feet,
While the red-white-and-blue was fluttering everywhere,
And the heart of the crowd kept time to a martial air:

O brave flag, O bright flag, O flag to lead the free!
The glory of thy silver stars,
Engrailed in blue above the bars
Of red for courage, white for truth,
Has brought the world a second youth
And drawn a hundred million hearts to follow after thee.

II

Old Cambridge saw thee first unfurled,
By Washington's far-reaching hand,
To greet, in Seventy-six, the wintry morn
Of a new year, and herald to the world

WHO FOLLOW THE FLAG

Glad tidings from a Western land,—
A people and a hope new-born!
The double cross then filled thine azure field,
In token of a spirit loath to yield
The breaking ties that bound thee to a throne.
But not for long thine oriflamme could bear
That symbol of an outworn trust in kings.
The wind that bore thee out on widening wings
Called for a greater sign and all thine own,—
A new device to speak of heavenly laws
And lights that surely guide the people's cause.
Oh, greatly did they hope, and greatly dare,
Who bade the stars in heaven fight for them,
And set upon their battle-flag a fair
New constellation as a diadem!
Along the blood-stained banks of Brandywine
The ragged troops were rallied to this sign;
Through Saratoga's woods it fluttered bright
Amid the perils of the hard-won fight;
O'er Yorktown's meadows broad and green
It hailed the glory of the final scene;
And when at length Manhattan saw
The last invaders' line of scarlet coats
Pass Bowling Green, and fill the waiting boats
And sullenly withdraw,
The flag that proudly flew
Above the battered line of buff and blue,
Marching, with rattling drums and shrilling pipes,

PRO PATRIA

Along the Bowery and down Broadway,
Was this that leads the great parade to-day,—
The glorious banner of the stars and stripes.

First of the flags of earth to dare
A heraldry so high;
First of the flags of earth to bear
The blazons of the sky;
Long may thy constellation glow,
Foretelling happy fate;
Wider thy starry circle grow,
And every star a State!

III

Pass on, pass on, ye flashing files
Of men who march in militant array;
Ye thrilling bugles, throbbing drums,
Ring out, roll on, and die away;
And fade, ye crowds, with the fading day!
Around the city's lofty piles
Of steel and stone
The lilac veil of dusk is thrown,
Entangled full of sparks of fairy light;
And the never-silent heart of the city hums
To a homeward-turning tune before the night.
But far above, on the sky-line's broken height,
From all the towers and domes outlined

In gray and gold along the city's crest,
I see the rippling flag still take the wind
With a promise of good to come for all mankind.

IV

O banner of the west,
No proud and brief parade,
That glorifies a nation's holiday
With show of troops for warfare dressed,
Can rightly measure or display
The mighty army thou hast made
Loyal to guard thy more than royal sway.
Millions have come across the sea
To find beneath thy shelter room to grow;
Millions were born beneath thy folds and know
No other flag but thee.
And other, darker millions bore the yoke
Of bondage in thy borders till the voice
Of Lincoln spoke,
And sent thee forth to set the bondmen free.
Rejoice, dear flag, rejoice!
Since thou hast proved and passed that bitter strife,
Richer thy red with blood of heroes wet,
Purer thy white through sacrificial life,
Brighter thy blue wherein new stars are set.
Thou art become a sign,
Revealed in heaven to speak of things divine:

Of Truth that dares
To slay the lie it sheltered unawares;
Of Courage fearless in the fight,
Yet ever quick its foemen to forgive;
Of Conscience earnest to maintain its right
And gladly grant the same to all who live.
Thy staff is deeply planted in the fact
That nothing can ennoble man
Save his own act,
And naught can make him worthy to be free
But practice in the school of liberty.
The cords are two that lift thee to the sky:
Firm faith in God, the King who rules on high;
And never-failing trust
In human nature, full of faults and flaws,
Yet ever answering to the inward call
That bids it set the "ought" above the "must,"
In all its errors wiser than it seems,
In all its failures full of generous dreams,
Through endless conflict rising without pause
To self-dominion, charactered in laws
That pledge fair-play alike to great and small,
And equal rights for each beneath the rule of all.
These are thy halyards, banner bold,
And while these hold,
Thy brightness from the sky shall never fall,
Thy broadening empire never know decrease,—
Thy strength is union and thy glory peace.

WHO FOLLOW THE FLAG

V

Look forth across thy widespread lands,
O flag, and let thy stars to-night be eyes
    To see the visionary hosts
Of men and women grateful to be thine,
    That joyfully arise
From all thy borders and thy coasts,
And follow after thee in endless line!
They lift to thee a forest of saluting hands;
They hail thee with a rolling ocean-roar
    Of cheers; and as the echo dies,
There comes a sweet and moving song
Of treble voices from the childish throng
Who run to thee from every school-house door.
Behold thine army! Here thy power lies:
The men whom freedom has made strong,
And bound to follow thee by willing vows;
    The women greatened by the joys
Of motherhood to rule a happy house;
    The vigorous girls and boys,
Whose eager faces and unclouded brows
Foretell the future of a noble race,
Rich in the wealth of wisdom and true worth!
While millions such as these to thee belong,
    What foe can do thee wrong,
What jealous rival rob thee of thy place
    Foremost of all the flags of earth?

PRO PATRIA

VI

My vision darkens as the night descends;
And through the mystic atmosphere
I feel the creeping coldness that portends
    A change of spirit in my dream
The multitude that moved with song and cheer
    Have vanished, yet a living stream
    Flows on and follows still the flag,
But silent now, with leaden feet that lag
    And falter in the deepening gloom,—
A weird battalion bringing up the rear.
Ah, who are these on whom the vital bloom
Of life has withered to the dust of doom?
These little pilgrims prematurely worn
And bent as if they bore the weight of years?
These childish faces, pallid and forlorn,
Too dull for laughter and too hard for tears?
Is this the ghost of that insane crusade
That led ten thousand children long ago,
A flock of innocents, deceived, betrayed,
Yet pressing on through want and woe
To meet their fate, faithful and unafraid?
    Nay, for a million children now
Are marching in the long pathetic line,
With weary step and early wrinkled brow;
And at their head appears no holy sign
    Of hope in heaven;
    For unto them is given

WHO FOLLOW THE FLAG

No cross to carry, but a cross to drag.
Before their strength is ripe they bear
The load of labour, toiling underground
In dangerous mines and breathing heavy air
Of crowded shops; their tender lives are bound
To service of the whirling, clattering wheels
That fill the factories with dust and noise;
    They are not girls and boys,
But little "hands" who blindly, dumbly feed
With their own blood the hungry god of Greed.
    Robbed of their natural joys,
And wounded with a scar that never heals,
They stumble on with heavy-laden soul,
And fall by thousands on the highway lined
With little graves; or reach at last their goal
Of stunted manhood and embittered age,
To brood awhile with dark and troubled mind,
Beside the smouldering fire of sullen rage,
On life's unfruitful work and niggard wage.
Are these the regiments that Freedom rears
    To serve her cause in coming years?
Nay, every life that Avarice doth maim
And beggar in the helpless days of youth,
    Shall surely claim
A just revenge, and take it without ruth;
And every soul denied the right to grow
Beneath the flag, shall be its secret foe.
Bow down, dear land, in penitence and shame!

PRO PATRIA

Remember now thine oath, so nobly sworn,
    To guard an equal lot
For every child within thy borders born!
These are thy children whom thou hast forgot:
They have the bitter right to live, but not
The blessed right to look for happiness.
O lift thy liberating hand once more,
To loose thy little ones from dark duress;
The vital gladness to their hearts restore
In healthful lessons and in happy play;
And set them free to climb the upward way
That leads to self-reliant nobleness.
Speak out, my country, speak at last,
    As thou hast spoken in the past,
    And clearly, bravely say:
    "I will defend
"The coming race on whom my hopes depend:
"Beneath my flag and on my sacred soil
"No child shall bear the crushing yoke of toil."

WHO FOLLOW THE FLAG

VII

Look up, look up, ye downcast eyes!
    The night is almost gone:
Along the new horizon flies
    The banner of the dawn;
The eastern sky is banded low
    With white and crimson bars,
While far above the morning glow
    The everlasting stars.

O bright flag, O brave flag, O flag to lead the free!
  The hand of God thy colours blent,
  And heaven to earth thy glory lent,
  To shield the weak, and guide the strong
  To make an end of human wrong,
And draw a countless human host to follow after thee!

STAIN NOT THE SKY

Ye gods of battle, lords of fear,
  Who work your iron will as well
As once ye did with sword and spear,
  With rifled gun and rending shell,—
Masters of sea and land, forbear
The fierce invasion of the inviolate air!

With patient daring man hath wrought
  A hundred years for power to fly;
And will you make his wingéd thought
  A hovering horror in the sky,
Where flocks of human eagles sail,
Dropping their bolts of death on hill and dale?

Ah no, the sunset is too pure,
  The dawn too fair, the noon too bright
For wings of terror to obscure
  Their beauty, and betray the night
That keeps for man, above his wars,
The tranquil vision of untroubled stars.

STAIN NOT THE SKY

Pass on, pass on, ye lords of fear!
  Your footsteps in the sea are red,
And black on earth your paths appear
  With ruined homes and heaps of dead.
Pass on to end your transient reign,
And leave the blue of heaven without a stain.

The wrong ye wrought will fall to dust,
  The right ye shielded will abide;
The world at last will learn to trust
  In law to guard, and love to guide;
And Peace of God that answers prayer
Will fall like dew from the inviolate air.

March 5, 1914.

PEACE-HYMN OF THE REPUBLIC

O Lord our God, Thy mighty hand
Hath made our country free;
From all her broad and happy land
May praise arise to Thee.
Fulfill the promise of her youth,
Her liberty defend;
By law and order, love and truth,
America befriend!

The strength of every State increase
In Union's golden chain;
Her thousand cities fill with peace,
Her million fields with grain.
The virtues of her mingled blood
In one new people blend;
By unity and brotherhood,
America befriend!

PEACE-HYMN OF THE REPUBLIC

O suffer not her feet to stray;
But guide her untaught might,
That she may walk in peaceful day,
And lead the world in light.
Bring down the proud, lift up the poor,
Unequal ways amend;
By justice, nation-wide and sure,
America befriend!

Thro' all the waiting land proclaim
Thy gospel of good-will;
And may the music of Thy name
In every bosom thrill.
O'er hill and vale, from sea to sea,
Thy holy reign extend;
By faith and hope and charity,
America befriend!

THE RED FLOWER
AND
GOLDEN STARS

These verses were written during the terrible world-war, and immediately after. The earlier ones had to be unsigned because America was still "neutral" and I held a diplomatic post. The rest of them were printed after I had resigned, and was free to speak out, and to take active service in the Navy, when America entered the great conflict for liberty and peace on earth.

Avalon, February 22, 1920.

THE RED FLOWER

June, 1914

In the pleasant time of Pentecost,
  By the little river Kyll,
I followed the angler's winding path
  Or waded the stream at will,
And the friendly fertile German land
  Lay round me green and still.

But all day long on the eastern bank
  Of the river cool and clear,
Where the curving track of the double rails
  Was hardly seen though near,
The endless trains of German troops
  Went rolling down to Trier.

They packed the windows with bullet heads
  And caps of hodden gray;
They laughed and sang and shouted loud
  When the trains were brought to a stay;
They waved their hands and sang again
  As they went on their iron way.

THE RED FLOWER

No shadow fell on the smiling land,
  No cloud arose in the sky;
I could hear the river's quiet tune
  When the trains had rattled by;
But my heart sank low with a heavy sense
  Of trouble,—I knew not why.

Then came I into a certain field
  Where the devil's paint-brush spread
'Mid the gray and green of the rolling hills
  A flaring splotch of red,—
An evil omen, a bloody sign,
  And a token of many dead.

I saw in a vision the field-gray horde
  Break forth at the devil's hour,
And trample the earth into crimson mud
  In the rage of the Will to Power,—
All this I dreamed in the valley of Kyll,
  At the sign of the blood-red flower.

A SCRAP OF PAPER

"Will you go to war just for a scrap of paper?"—*Question of the German Chancellor to the British Ambassador, August 5,* 1914.

A MOCKING question! Britain's answer came
Swift as the light and searching as the flame.

"Yes, for a scrap of paper we will fight
Till our last breath, and God defend the right!

"A scrap of paper where a name is set
Is strong as duty's pledge and honor's debt.

"A scrap of paper holds for man and wife
The sacrament of love, the bond of life.

"A scrap of paper may be Holy Writ
With God's eternal word to hallow it.

"A scrap of paper binds us both to stand
Defenders of a neutral neighbor land.

"By God, by faith, by honor, yes! We fight
To keep our name upon that paper white."

September, 1914.

STAND FAST

STAND fast, Great Britain!
Together England, Scotland, Ireland stand
One in the faith that makes a mighty land,—
True to the bond you gave and will not break
And fearless in the fight for conscience' sake!
Against the Giant Robber clad in steel,
With blood of trampled Belgium on his heel,
Striding through France to strike you down at last,
Britain, stand fast!

Stand fast, brave land!
The Huns are thundering toward the citadel;
They prate of Culture but their path is Hell;
Their light is darkness, and the bloody sword
They wield and worship is their only Lord.
O land where reason stands secure on right,
O land where freedom is the source of light,
Against the mailed Barbarians' deadly blast,
Britain, stand fast!

STAND FAST

Stand fast, dear land!
Thou island mother of a world-wide race,
Whose children speak thy tongue and love thy face,
Their hearts and hopes are with thee in the strife,
Their hands will break the sword that seeks thy life;
Fight on until the Teuton madness cease;
Fight bravely on, until the word of peace
Is spoken in the English tongue at last,—
Britain, stand fast!

September, 1914.

LIGHTS OUT

(1915)

"Lights out" along the land,
"Lights out" upon the sea.
The night must put her hiding hand
O'er peaceful towns where children sleep,
And peaceful ships that darkly creep
Across the waves, as if they were not free.

The dragons of the air,
The hell-hounds of the deep,
Lurking and prowling everywhere,
Go forth to seek their helpless prey,
Not knowing whom they maim or slay—
Mad harvesters, who care not what they reap.

Out with the tranquil lights,
Out with the lights that burn
For love and law and human rights!
Set back the clock a thousand years:
All they have gained now disappears,
And the dark ages suddenly return.

LIGHTS OUT

Kaiser, who loosed wild death,
And terror in the night,
God grant you draw no quiet breath,
Until the madness you began
Is ended, and long-suffering man,
Set free from war lords, cries, "Let there be Light."

October, 1915.

Read at the meeting of the American Academy, Boston, November, 1915.

REMARKS ABOUT KINGS

"*God said I am tired of kings.*"—EMERSON.

GOD said, "I am tired of kings,"—
But that was a long while ago!
And meantime man said, "No,—
I like their looks in their robes and rings."
So he crowned a few more,
And they went on playing the game as before,
Fighting and spoiling things.

Man said, "I am tired of kings!
Sons of the robber-chiefs of yore,
They make me pay for their lust and their war;
I am the puppet, they pull the strings;
The blood of my heart is the wine they drink.
I will govern myself for awhile I think,
And see what that brings!"

Then God, who made the first remark,
Smiled in the dark.

October, 1915.

Read at the meeting of the American Academy, Boston, November, 1915.

MIGHT AND RIGHT

If Might made Right, life were a wild-beasts' cage;
If Right made Might, this were the golden age;
But now, until we win the long campaign,
Right must gain Might to conquer and to reign.

July 1, 1915.

THE PRICE OF PEACE

Peace without Justice is a low estate,—
A coward cringing to an iron Fate!
But Peace through Justice is the great ideal,—
We'll pay the price of war to make it real.

December 28, 1916.

STORM-MUSIC

O MUSIC hast thou only heard
The laughing river, the singing bird,
The murmuring wind in the poplar-trees,—
Nothing but Nature's melodies?
  Nay, thou hearest all her tones,
    As a Queen must hear!
    Sounds of wrath and fear,
    Mutterings, shouts, and moans,
  Madness, tumult, and despair,—
  All she has that shakes the air
  With voices fierce and wild!
Thou art a Queen and not a dreaming child,—
Put on thy crown and let us hear thee reign
Triumphant in a world of storm and strain!

  Echo the long-drawn sighs
Of the mounting wind in the pines;
And the sobs of the mounting waves that rise
  In the dark of the troubled deep
To break on the beach in fiery lines.
  Echo the far-off roll of thunder,
      Rumbling loud
  And ever louder, under
  The blue-black curtain of cloud,
  Where the lightning serpents gleam.

STORM-MUSIC

Echo the moaning
Of the forest in its sleep
Like a giant groaning
In the torment of a dream.

Now an interval of quiet
For a moment holds the air
In the breathless hush
Of a silent prayer.

Then the sudden rush
Of the rain, and the riot
Of the shrieking, tearing gale
Breaks loose in the night,
With a fusillade of hail!
Hear the forest fight,
With its tossing arms that crack and clash
In the thunder's cannonade,
While the lightning's forkèd flash
Brings the old hero-trees to the ground with a crash!
Hear the breakers' deepening roar,
Driven like a herd of cattle
In the wild stampede of battle,
Trampling, trampling, trampling, to overwhelm the shore!

THE RED FLOWER

Is it the end of all?
Will the land crumble and fall?
Nay, for a voice replies
Out of the hidden skies,
"Thus far, O sea, shalt thou go,
So long, O wind, shalt thou blow:
Return to your bounds and cease,
And let the earth have peace!"

O Music, lead the way—
The stormy night is past,
Lift up our hearts to greet the day,
And the joy of things that last.

The dissonance and pain
That mortals must endure,
Are changed in thine immortal strain
To something great and pure.

True love will conquer strife,
And strength from conflict flows,
For discord is the thorn of life
And harmony the rose.

May, 1916.

THE BELLS OF MALINES

August 17, 1914

THE gabled roofs of old Malines
Are russet red and gray and green,
And o'er them in the sunset hour
Looms, dark and huge, St. Rombold's tower.
High in that rugged nest concealed,
The sweetest bells that ever pealed,
The deepest bells that ever rung,
The lightest bells that ever sung,
Are waiting for the master's hand
To fling their music o'er the land.

And shall they ring to-night, Malines?
In nineteen hundred and fourteen,
The frightful year, the year of woe,
When fire and blood and rapine flow
Across the land from lost Liége,
Storm-driven by the German rage?
The other carillons have ceased:
Fallen is Hasselt, fallen Diest,
From Ghent and Bruges no voices come,
Antwerp is silent, Brussels dumb!

THE RED FLOWER

But in thy belfry, O Malines,
The master of the bells unseen
Has climbed to where the keyboard stands,—
To-night his heart is in his hands!
Once more, before invasion's hell
Breaks round the tower he loves so well,
Once more he strikes the well-worn keys,
And sends aërial harmonies
Far-floating through the twilight dim
In patriot song and holy hymn.

O listen, burghers of Malines!
Soldier and workman, pale béguine,
And mother with a trembling flock
Of children clinging to thy frock,—
Look up and listen, listen all!
What tunes are these that gently fall
Around you like a benison?
"The Flemish Lion," "Brabançonne,"
"O brave Liége," and all the airs
That Belgium in her bosom bears.

Ring up, ye silvery octaves high,
Whose notes like circling swallows fly;
And ring, each old sonorous bell,—
"Jesu," "Maria," "Michaël!"

THE BELLS OF MALINES

Weave in and out, and high and low,
The magic music that you know,
And let it float and flutter down
To cheer the heart of the troubled town.
Ring out, "Salvator," lord of all,—
"Roland" in Ghent may hear thee call!

O brave bell-music of Malines,
In this dark hour how much you mean!
The dreadful night of blood and tears
Sweeps down on Belgium, but she hears
Deep in her heart the melody
Of songs she learned when she was free.
She will not falter, faint, nor fail,
But fight until her rights prevail
And all her ancient belfries ring
"The Flemish Lion," "God Save the King!"

JEANNE D'ARC RETURNS*

1914–1916

WHAT hast thou done, O womanhood of France,
  Mother and daughter, sister, sweetheart, wife,
  What hast thou done, amid this fateful strife,
To prove the pride of thine inheritance
In this fair land of freedom and romance?
  I hear thy voice with tears and courage rife,—
  Smiling against the swords that seek thy life,—
Make answer in a noble utterance:
"I give France all I have, and all she asks.
  Would it were more! Ah, let her ask and take:
My hands to nurse her wounded, do her tasks,—
  My feet to run her errands through the dark,—
My heart to bleed in triumph for her sake,—
  And all my soul to follow thee, Jeanne d'Arc!"

April 16, 1916.

* This sonnet belongs with the poem on page 309, " Come Back Again, Jeanne D'Arc."

THE NAME OF FRANCE

GIVE us a name to fill the mind
With the shining thoughts that lead mankind,
The glory of learning, the joy of art,—
A name that tells of a splendid part
In the long, long toil and the strenuous fight
Of the human race to win its way
From the feudal darkness into the day
Of Freedom, Brotherhood, Equal Right,—
A name like a star, a name of light.
I give you *France!*

Give us a name to stir the blood
With a warmer glow and a swifter flood,
At the touch of a courage that conquers fear,—
A name like the sound of a trumpet, clear,
And silver-sweet, and iron-strong,
That calls three million men to their feet,
Ready to march, and steady to meet
The foes who threaten that name with wrong,—
A name that rings like a battle-song.
I give you *France!*

THE RED FLOWER

Give us a name to move the heart
With the strength that noble griefs impart,
A name that speaks of the blood outpoured
To save mankind from the sway of the sword,—
A name that calls on the world to share
In the burden of sacrificial strife
When the cause at stake is the world's free life
And the rule of the people everywhere,—
A name like a vow, a name like a prayer.
I give you *France!*

The Hague, September, 1916.

AMERICA'S PROSPERITY

THEY tell me thou art rich, my country: gold
  In glittering flood has poured into thy chest;
  Thy flocks and herds increase, thy barns are pressed
With harvest, and thy stores can hardly hold
Their merchandise; unending trains are rolled
  Along thy network rails of East and West;
  Thy factories and forges never rest;
Thou art enriched in all things bought and sold!

But dost *thou* prosper? Better news I crave.
  O dearest country, is it well with thee
    Indeed, and is thy soul in health?
A nobler people, hearts more wisely brave,
  And thoughts that lift men up and make them free,—
    These are prosperity and vital wealth!

The Hague, October 1, 1916.

THE GLORY OF SHIPS

THE glory of ships is an old, old song,
  since the days when the sea-rovers ran,
In their open boats through the roaring surf,
  and the spread of the world began;
The glory of ships is a light on the sea,
  and a star in the story of man.

When Homer sang of the galleys of Greece
  that conquered the Trojan shore,
And Solomon lauded the barks of Tyre
  that brought great wealth to his door,
'Twas little they knew, those ancient men,
  what would come of the sail and the oar.

The Greek ships rescued the West from the East,
  when they harried the Persians home;
And the Roman ships were the wings of strength
  that bore up the empire, Rome;
And the ships of Spain found a wide new world,
  far over the fields of foam.

THE GLORY OF SHIPS

Then the tribes of courage at last saw clear
that the ocean was not a bound,
But a broad highway, and a challenge to seek
for treasure as yet unfound;
So the fearless ships fared forth to the search,
in joy that the globe was round.

Their hulls were heightened, their sails spread out,
they grew with the growth of their quest;
They opened the secret doors of the East,
and the golden gates of the West;
And many a city of high renown
was proud of a ship on its crest.

The fleets of England and Holland and France
were at strife with each other and Spain;
And battle and storm sent a myriad ships
to sleep in the depths of the main;
But the seafaring spirit could never be drowned,
and it filled up the fleets again.

They greatened and grew, with the aid of steam,
to a wonderful, vast array,
That carries the thoughts and the traffic of men
into every harbor and bay;
And now in the world-wide work of the ships
'tis England that leads the way.

THE RED FLOWER

O well for the leading that follows the law
of a common right on the sea!
But ill for the leader who tries to hold
what belongs to mankind in fee!
The way of the ships is an open way,
and the ocean must ever be free!

Remember, O first of the maritime folk,
how the rise of your greatness began.
It will live if you safeguard the round-the-world road
from the shame of a selfish ban;
For the glory of ships is a light on the sea,
and a star in the story of man!

September 12, 1916.

MARE LIBERUM

I

You dare to say with perjured lips,
"We fight to make the ocean free"?
You, whose black trail of butchered ships
Bestrews the bed of every sea
Where German submarines have wrought
Their horrors! Have you never thought,—
What you call freedom, men call piracy!

II

Unnumbered ghosts that haunt the wave,
Where you have murdered, cry you down;
And seamen whom you would not save,
Weave now in weed-grown depths a crown
Of shame for your imperious head,
A dark memorial of the dead
Women and children whom you sent to drown.

THE RED FLOWER

III

Nay, not till thieves are set to guard
The gold, and corsairs called to keep
O'er peaceful commerce watch and ward,
And wolves to herd the helpless sheep,
Shall men and women look to thee,
Thou ruthless Old Man of the Sea,
To safeguard law and freedom on the deep!

IV

In nobler breeds we put our trust:
The nations in whose sacred lore
The "Ought" stands out above the "Must,"
And honor rules in peace and war.
With these we hold in soul and heart,
With these we choose our lot and part,
Till Liberty is safe on sea and shore.

London Times, February 12, 1917.

"LIBERTY ENLIGHTENING THE WORLD"

Thou warden of the western gate, above Manhattan
Bay,
The fogs of doubt that hid thy face are driven clean
away:
Thine eyes at last look far and clear, thou liftest high
thy hand
To spread the light of liberty world-wide for every land.

No more thou dreamest of a peace reserved alone for
thee,
While friends are fighting for thy cause beyond the
guardian sea:
The battle that they wage is thine; thou fallest if they
fall;
The swollen flood of Prussian pride will sweep unchecked
o'er all.

O cruel is the conquer-lust in Hohenzollern brains:
The paths they plot to gain their goal are dark with
shameful stains;
No faith they keep, no law revere, no god but naked
Might;
They are the foemen of mankind. Up, Liberty, and
smite!

THE RED FLOWER

Britain, and France, and Italy, and Russia newly born,
Have waited for thee in the night. Oh, come as comes
the morn!
Serene and strong and full of faith, America, arise,
With steady hope and mighty help to join thy brave
Allies.

O dearest country of my heart, home of the high desire,
Make clean thy soul for sacrifice on Freedom's altar-
fire:
For thou must suffer, thou must fight, until the war-
lords cease,
And all the peoples lift their heads in liberty and peace.

London Times, April 12, 1917.

THE OXFORD THRUSHES

February, 1917

I NEVER thought again to hear
The Oxford thrushes singing clear,
Amid the February rain,
Their sweet, indomitable strain.

A wintry vapor lightly spreads
Among the trees, and round the beds
Where daffodil and jonquil sleep;
Only the snowdrop wakes to weep.

It is not springtime yet. Alas,
What dark, tempestuous days must pass,
Till England's trial by battle cease,
And summer comes again with peace.

The lofty halls, the tranquil towers,
Where Learning in untroubled hours
Held her high court, serene in fame,
Are lovely still, yet not the same.

The novices in fluttering gown
No longer fill the ancient town;
But fighting men in khaki drest,
And in the Schools the wounded rest.

THE RED FLOWER

Ah, far away, 'neath stranger skies
Full many a son of Oxford lies,
And whispers from his warrior grave,
"I died to keep the faith you gave."

The mother mourns, but does not fail,
Her courage and her love prevail
O'er sorrow, and her spirit hears
The promise of triumphant years.

Then sing, ye thrushes, in the rain
Your sweet indomitable strain.
Ye bring a word from God on high
And voices in our hearts reply.

HOMEWARD BOUND

HOME, for my heart still calls me;
  Home, through the danger zone;
Home, whatever befalls me,
  I will sail again to my own!

Wolves of the sea are hiding
  Closely along the way,
Under the water biding
  Their moment to rend and slay.

Black is the eagle that brands them,
  Black are their hearts as the night,
Black is the hate that sends them
  To murder but not to fight.

Flower of the German Culture,
  Boast of the Kaiser's Marine,
Choose for your emblem the vulture,
  Cowardly, cruel, obscene!

Forth from her sheltered haven
  Our peaceful ship glides slow,
Noiseless in flight as a raven,
  Gray as a hoodie crow.

THE RED FLOWER

She doubles and turns in her bearing,
  Like a twisting plover she goes;
The way of her westward faring
  Only the captain knows.

In a lonely bay concealing
  She lingers for days, and slips
At dusk from her covert, stealing
  Thro' channels feared by the ships.

Brave are the men, and steady,
  Who guide her over the deep,—
British mariners, ready
  To face the sea-wolf's leap.

Lord of the winds and waters,
  Bring our ship to her mark,
Safe from this game of hide-and-seek
  With murderers in the dark!

On the S. S. *Baltic*, May, 1917.

THE WINDS OF WAR-NEWS

THE winds of war-news change and veer:
Now westerly and full of cheer,
Now easterly, depressing, sour
With tidings of the Teutons' power.

But thou, America, whose heart
With brave Allies has taken part,
Be not a weathercock to change
With these wild winds that shift and range.

Be thou a compass ever true,
Through sullen clouds or skies of blue,
To that great star which rules the night,—
The star of Liberty and Right.

Lover of peace, oh set thy soul,
Thy strength, thy wealth, thy conscience whole,
To win the peace thine eyes foresee,—
The triumph of Democracy.

December 19, 1917.

RIGHTEOUS WRATH

THERE are many kinds of anger, as many kinds of fire;
And some are fierce and fatal with murderous desire;
And some are mean and craven, revengeful, sullen, slow,
They hurt the man that holds them more than they
hurt his foe.

And yet there is an anger that purifies the heart:
The anger of the better against the baser part,
Against the false and wicked, against the tyrant's sword,
Against the enemies of love, and all that hate the Lord.

O cleansing indignation, O flame of righteous wrath,
Give me a soul to feel thee and follow in thy path!
Save me from selfish virtue, arm me for fearless fight,
And give me strength to carry on, a soldier of the Right!

January, 1918.

THE PEACEFUL WARRIOR

I HAVE no joy in strife,
  Peace is my great desire;
Yet God forbid I lose my life
  Through fear to face the fire.

A peaceful man must fight
  For that which peace demands,—
Freedom and faith, honor and right,
  Defend with heart and hands.

Farewell, my friendly books;
  Farewell, ye woods and streams;
The fate that calls me forward looks
  To a duty beyond dreams.

Oh, better to be dead
  With a face turned to the sky,
Than live beneath a slavish dread
  And serve a giant lie.

Stand up, my heart, and strive
  For the things most dear to thee!
Why should we care to be alive
  Unless the world is free?

May, 1918.

FROM GLORY UNTO GLORY

AMERICAN FLAG SONG

1776

O DARK the night and dim the day
  When first our flag arose;
It fluttered bravely in the fray
  To meet o'erwhelming foes.
Our fathers saw the splendor shine,
  They dared and suffered all;
They won our freedom by the sign—
The holy sign, the radiant sign—
  Of the stars that never fall.

Chorus

All hail to thee, Young Glory!
  Among the flags of earth
We'll ne'er forget the story
  Of thy heroic birth.

1861

O wild the later storm that shook
  The pillars of the State,
When brother against brother took
  The final arms of fate.
But union lived and peace divine
  Enfolded brothers all;

FROM GLORY UNTO GLORY

The flag floats o'er them with the sign—
The loyal sign, the equal sign—
  Of the stars that never fall.

Chorus

All hail to thee, Old Glory!
  Of thee our heart's desire
Foretells a golden story,
  For thou hast come through fire.

1917

O fiercer than all wars before
  That raged on land or sea,
The Giant Robber's world-wide war
  For the things that shall not be!
Thy sister banners hold the line;
  To thee, dear flag, they call;
And thou hast joined them with the sign—
The heavenly sign, the victor sign—
  Of the stars that never fall.

Chorus

All hail to thee, New Glory!
  We follow thee unfurled
To write the larger story
  Of Freedom for the World.

September 4, 1918.

BRITAIN, FRANCE, AMERICA

THE rough expanse of democratic sea
Which parts the lands that live by liberty
Is no division; for their hearts are one.
To fight together till their cause is won.

For land and water let us make our pact,
And seal the solemn word with valiant act:
No continent is firm, no ocean pure,
Until on both the rights of man are sure.

April, 1917.

THE RED CROSS

SIGN of the Love Divine
  That bends to bear the load
Of all who suffer, all who bleed,
  Along life's thorny road:

Sign of the Heart Humane,
  That through the darkest fight
Would bring to wounded friend and foe
  A ministry of light:

O dear and holy sign,
  Lead onward like a star!
The armies of the just are thine,
  And all we have and are.

October 20, 1918.
For the Red Cross Christmas Roll Call.

EASTER ROAD

1918

UNDER the cloud of world-wide war,
While earth is drenched with sorrow,
I have no heart for idle merrymaking,
Or for the fashioning of glad raiment.
I will retrace the divine footmarks,
On the Road of the first Easter

Down through the valley of utter darkness
Dripping with blood and tears;
Over the hill of the skull, the little hill of great anguish,
The ambuscade of Death.
Into the no-man's-land of Hades
Bearing despatches of hope to spirits in prison,
Mortally stricken and triumphant
Went the faithful Captain of Salvation.

Then upward, swiftly upward,—
Victory, liberty, glory,
The feet that were wounded walked in the tranquil garden,
Bathed in dew and the light of deathless dawn.

O my soul, my comrades, soldiers of freedom,
Follow the pathway of Easter, for there is no other,

EASTER ROAD

Follow it through to peace, yea, follow it fighting.
This Armageddon is not darker than Calvary.
The day will break when the Dragon is vanquished;
He that exalteth himself as God shall be cast down,
And the Lords of war shall fall,
And the long, long terror be ended,
Victory, justice, peace enduring!
They that die in this cause shall live forever,
And they that live shall never die,
They shall rejoice together in the Easter of a new world.

March 31, 1918.

AMERICA'S WELCOME HOME

Oh, gallantly they fared forth in khaki and in blue,
America's crusading host of warriors bold and true;
They battled for the rights of man beside our brave Allies,
And now they're coming home to us with glory in their eyes.

Oh, it's home again, and home again, America for me!
Our hearts are turning home again and there we long to be,
In our beautiful big country beyond the ocean bars,
Where the air is full of sunlight and the flag is full of stars.

Our boys have seen the Old World as none have seen before.
They know the grisly horror of the German gods of war:
The noble faith of Britain and the hero-heart of France,
The soul of Belgium's fortitude and Italy's romance.

They bore our country's great word across the rolling sea,
"America swears brotherhood with all the just and free."
They wrote that word victorious on fields of mortal strife,
And many a valiant lad was proud to seal it with his life.

AMERICA'S WELCOME HOME

Oh, welcome home in Heaven's peace, dear spirits of the dead!
And welcome home ye living sons America hath bred!
The lords of war are beaten down, your glorious task is done;
You fought to make the whole world free, and the victory is won.

Now it's home again, and home again, our hearts are turning west,
Of all the lands beneath the sun America is best.
We're going home to our own folks, beyond the ocean bars,
Where the air is full of sunlight and the flag is full of stars.

November 11, 1918.
A sequel to "America For Me," written in 1909. Page 314.

THE SURRENDER OF THE GERMAN FLEET

SHIP after ship, and every one with a high-resounding name,
From the robber-nest of Heligoland the German warfleet came;
Not victory or death they sought, but a rendezvous of shame.

Sing out, sing out,
A joyful shout,
Ye lovers of the sea!
The "Kaiser" and the "Kaiserin,"
The "König" and the "Prinz,"
The potentates of piracy,
Are coming to surrender,
And the ocean shall be free.

They never dared the final fate of battle on the blue;
Their sea-wolves murdered merchantmen and mocked the drowning crew;
They stained the wave with martyr-blood,—but we sent our transports through!

SURRENDER OF THE GERMAN FLEET

What flags are these that dumbly droop from the gaff o' the mainmast tall?
The black of the Kaiser's iron cross, the red of the Empire's fall!
Come down, come down, ye pirate flags. Yea, strike your colors all.

The Union Jack and the Tricolor and the Starry Flag o' the West
Shall guard the fruit of Freedom's war and the victory confest,
The flags of the brave and just and free shall rule on the ocean's breast.

Sing out, sing out,
A mighty shout,
Ye lovers of the sea!
The "Kaiser" and the "Kaiserin,"
The "König" and the "Prinz,"
The robber-lords of death and sin,
Have come to their surrender,
And the ocean shall be free!

November 20, 1918.

GOLDEN STARS

I

It was my lot of late to travel far
Through all America's domain,
A willing, gray-haired servitor
Bearing the Fiery Cross of righteous war.
And everywhere, on mountain, vale and plain,
In crowded street and lonely cottage door,
I saw the symbol of the bright blue star.
Millions of stars! Rejoice, dear land, rejoice
That God hath made thee great enough to give
Beneath thy starry flag unfurled
A gift to all the world,—
Thy living sons that Liberty might live.

II

It seems but yesterday they sallied forth
Boys of the east, the west, the south, the north,
High-hearted, keen, with laughter and with song,
Fearless of lurking danger on the sea,
Eager to fight in Flanders or in France
Against the monstrous German wrong,
And sure of victory!
Brothers in soul with British and with French

They held their ground in many a bloody trench;
And when the swift word came—
Advance!
Over the top they went through waves of flame,—
Confident, reckless, irresistible,
Real Americans,—
Their rush was never stayed
Until the foe fell back, defeated and dismayed.
O land that bore them, write upon thy roll
Of battles won
To liberate the human soul,
Château Thierry and Saint Mihiel
And the fierce agony of the Argonne;
Yea, count among thy little rivers, dear
Because of friends whose feet have trodden there,
The Marne, the Meuse, and the Moselle.

III

Now the vile sword
In Potsdam forged and bathed in hell,
Is beaten down, the victory given
To the sword forged in faith and bathed in heaven.
Now home again our heroes come:
Oh, welcome them with bugle and with drum,
Ring bells, blow whistles, make a joyful noise
Unto the Lord,
And welcome home our blue-star boys,

Whose manhood has made known
To all the world America,
Unselfish, brave and free, the Great Republic,
Who lives not to herself alone.

IV

But many a lad we hold
Dear in our heart of hearts
Is missing from the home-returning host.
Ah, say not they are lost,
For they have found and given their life
In sacrificial strife:
Their service stars have changed from blue to gold!
That sudden rapture took them far away,
Yet are they here with us to-day,
Even as the heavenly stars we cannot see
Through the bright veil of sunlight,
Shed their influence still
On our vexed life, and promise peace
From God to all men of good will.

V

What wreaths shall we entwine
For our dear boys to deck their holy shrine?
  Mountain-laurel, morning-glory,
  Goldenrod and asters blue,
  Purple loosestrife, prince's-pine,

Wild-azalea, meadow-rue,
Nodding-lilies, columbine,—
All the native blooms that grew
In these fresh woods and pastures new,
Wherein they loved to ramble and to play.
Bring no exotic flowers:
America was in their hearts,
And they are ours
For ever and a day.

VI

O happy warriors, forgive the tear
Falling from eyes that miss you:
Forgive the word of grief from mother-lips
That ne'er on earth shall kiss you;
Hear only what our hearts would have you hear,—
Glory and praise and gratitude and pride
From the dear country in whose cause you died.
Now you have run your race and won your prize,
Old age shall never burden you, the fears
And conflicts that beset our lingering years
Shall never vex your souls in Paradise.
Immortal, young, and crowned with victory,
From life's long battle you have found release.
And He who died for all on Calvary
Has welcomed you, brave soldiers of the cross,
Into eternal Peace.

GOLDEN STARS

VII

Come, let us gird our loins and lift our load,
Companions who are left on life's rough road,
And bravely take the way that we must tread
To keep true faith with our beloved dead.
To conquer war they dared their lives to give,
To safeguard peace our hearts must learn to live.
Help us, dear God, our forward faith to hold!
We want a better world than that of old.
Lead us on paths of high endeavor,
Toiling upward, climbing ever,
Ready to suffer for the right,
Until at last we gain a loftier height,
More worthy to behold
Our guiding stars, our hero-stars of gold.

Ode for the Memorial Service,
Princeton University, December 15, 1918.

IN THE BLUE HEAVEN

In the blue heaven the clouds will come and go,
Scudding before the gale, or drifting slow
As galleons becalmed in Sundown Bay:
And through the air the birds will wing their way
Soaring to far-off heights, or flapping low,
Or darting like an arrow from the bow;
And when the twilight comes the stars will show,
One after one, their tranquil bright array
In the blue heaven.

But ye who fearless flew to meet the foe,
Eagles of freedom,—nevermore, we know,
Shall we behold you floating far away.
Yet clouds and birds and every starry ray
Will draw our heart to where your spirits glow
In the blue Heaven.

For the American Aviators who died in the war.
March, 1919.

A SHRINE IN THE PANTHEON

FOR THE UNNAMED SOLDIERS WHO DIED IN FRANCE

Universal approval has been accorded the proposal made in the French Chamber that the ashes of an unnamed French soldier, fallen for his country, shall be removed with solemn ceremony to the Pantheon. In this way it is intended to honor by a symbolic ceremony the memory of all who lie in unmarked graves.

HERE the great heart of France,
Victor in noble strife,
Doth consecrate a Poilu's tomb
To those who saved her life.

Brave son without a name,
Your country calls you home,
To rest among her heirs of fame,
Beneath the Pantheon's dome!

Now from the height of Heaven,
The souls of heroes look;
Their names, ungraven on this stone,
Are written in God's book.

Women of France, who mourn
Your dead in unmarked ground,
Come hither! Here the man you loved
In the heart of France is found!

IN PRAISE OF POETS

MOTHER EARTH

MOTHER of all the high-strung poets and singers departed,
Mother of all the grass that weaves over their graves the glory of the field,
Mother of all the manifold forms of life, deep-bosomed, patient, impassive,
Silent brooder and nurse of lyrical joys and sorrows!
Out of thee, yea, surely out of the fertile depth below thy breast,
Issued in some strange way, thou lying motionless, voiceless,
All these songs of nature, rhythmical, passionate, yearning,
Coming in music from earth, but not unto earth returning.

Dust are the blood-red hearts that beat in time to these measures,
Thou hast taken them back to thyself, secretly, irresistibly
Drawing the crimson currents of life down, down, down
Deep into thy bosom again, as a river is lost in the sand.
But the souls of the singers have entered into the songs that revealed them,—
Passionate songs, immortal songs of joy and grief and love and longing,

IN PRAISE OF POETS

Floating from heart to heart of thy children, they echo
above thee:
Do they not utter thy heart, the voices of those that love
thee?

Long hadst thou lain like a queen transformed by some
old enchantment
Into an alien shape, mysterious, beautiful, speechless,
Knowing not who thou wert, till the touch of thy Lord
and Lover
Wakened the man-child within thee to tell thy secret.
All of thy flowers and birds and forests and flowing
waters
Are but the rhythmical forms to reveal the life of the
spirit;
Thou thyself, earth-mother, in mountain and meadow
and ocean,
Holdest the poem of God, eternal thought and emotion.

December, 1905.

MILTON

I

LOVER of beauty, walking on the height
  Of pure philosophy and tranquil song;
  Born to behold the visions that belong
To those who dwell in melody and light;
Milton, thou spirit delicate and bright!
  What drew thee down to join the Roundhead throng
  Of iron-sided warriors, rude and strong,
Fighting for freedom in a world half night?

Lover of Liberty at heart wast thou,
  Above all beauty bright, all music clear:
To thee she bared her bosom and her brow,
  Breathing her virgin promise in thine ear,
And bound thee to her with a double vow,—
  Exquisite Puritan, grave Cavalier!

II

The cause, the cause for which thy soul resigned
  Her singing robes to battle on the plain,
  Was won, O poet, and was lost again;
And lost the labour of thy lonely mind
On weary tasks of prose. What wilt thou find
  To comfort thee for all the toil and pain?
  What solace, now thy sacrifice is vain
And thou art left forsaken, poor, and blind?

Like organ-music comes the deep reply:
  "The cause of truth looks lost, but shall be won.
For God hath given to mine inward eye
  Vision of England soaring to the sun.
And granted me great peace before I die,
  In thoughts of lowly duty bravely done."

III

O bend again above thine organ-board,
  Thou blind old poet longing for repose!
  Thy Master claims thy service not with those
Who only stand and wait for His reward;
He pours the heavenly gift of song restored
  Into thy breast, and bids thee nobly close
  A noble life, with poetry that flows
In mighty music of the major chord.

Where hast thou learned this deep, majestic strain,
  Surpassing all thy youthful lyric grace,
To sing of Paradise? Ah, not in vain
  The griefs that won at Dante's side thy place,
And made thee, Milton, by thy years of pain,
  The loftiest poet of the English race!

1908.

WORDSWORTH

WORDSWORTH, thy music like a river rolls
  Among the mountains, and thy song is fed
  By living springs far up the watershed;
No whirling flood nor parching drought controls
The crystal current: even on the shoals
  It murmurs clear and sweet; and when its bed
  Deepens below mysterious cliffs of dread,
Thy voice of peace grows deeper in our souls.

But thou in youth hast known the breaking stress
  Of passion, and hast trod despair's dry ground
    Beneath black thoughts that wither and destroy.
Ah, wanderer, led by human tenderness
  Home to the heart of Nature, thou hast found
    The hidden Fountain of Recovered Joy.

October, 1906.

KEATS

THE melancholy gift Aurora gained
  From Jove, that her sad lover should not see
  The face of death, no goddess asked for thee,
My Keats! But when the scarlet blood-drop stained
Thy pillow, thou didst read the fate ordained,—
  Brief life, wild love, a flight of poesy!
  And then,—a shadow fell on Italy:
Thy star went down before its brightness waned.

Yet thou hast won the gift Tithonus missed:
  Never to feel the pain of growing old,
    Nor lose the blissful sight of beauty's truth,
But with the ardent lips Urania kissed
  To breathe thy song, and, ere thy heart grew cold,
    Become the Poet of Immortal Youth.

August, 1906.

SHELLEY

KNIGHT-ERRANT of the Never-ending Quest,
  And Minstrel of the Unfulfilled Desire;
  For ever tuning thy frail earthly lyre
To some unearthly music, and possessed
With painful passionate longing to invest
  The golden dream of Love's immortal fire
  With mortal robes of beautiful attire,
And fold perfection to thy throbbing breast!

What wonder, Shelley, that the restless wave
  Should claim thee and the leaping flame consume
    Thy drifted form on Viareggio's beach?
These were thine elements,—thy fitting grave.
  But still thy soul rides on with fiery plume,
    Thy wild song rings in ocean's yearning speech!

August, 1906.

ROBERT BROWNING

How blind the toil that burrows like the mole,
  In winding graveyard pathways underground,
  For Browning's lineage! What if men have found
Poor footmen or rich merchants on the roll
Of his forbears? Did they beget his soul?
  Nay, for he came of ancestry renowned
  Through all the world,—the poets laurel-crowned
With wreaths from which the autumn takes no toll.

The blazons on his coat-of-arms are these:
  The flaming sign of Shelley's heart on fire,
    The golden globe of Shakespeare's human stage,
    The staff and scrip of Chaucer's pilgrimage,
  The rose of Dante's deep, divine desire,
The tragic mask of wise Euripides.

November, 1906.

TENNYSON

In Lucem Transitus, October, 1892

From the misty shores of midnight, touched with splendours of the moon,
To the singing tides of heaven, and the light more clear than noon,
Passed a soul that grew to music till it was with God in tune.

Brother of the greatest poets, true to nature, true to art;
Lover of Immortal Love, uplifter of the human heart;
Who shall cheer us with high music, who shall sing, if thou depart?

Silence here—for love is silent, gazing on the lessening sail;
Silence here—for grief is voiceless when the mighty minstrels fail;
Silence here—but far beyond us, many voices crying, Hail!

"IN MEMORIAM"

THE record of a faith sublime,
  And hope, through clouds, far-off discerned;
  The incense of a love that burned
Through pain and doubt defying Time:

The story of a soul at strife
  That learned at last to kiss the rod,
  And passed through sorrow up to God,
From living to a higher life:

A light that gleams across the wave
  Of darkness, down the rolling years,
  Piercing the heavy mist of tears—
A rainbow shining o'er a grave.

VICTOR HUGO

1802–1902

HEART of France for a hundred years,
  Passionate, sensitive, proud, and strong,
Quick to throb with her hopes and fears,
  Fierce to flame with her sense of wrong!
  You, who hailed with a morning song
Dream-light gilding a throne of old:
You, who turned when the dream grew cold,
Singing still, to the light that shone
Pure from Liberty's ancient throne,
    Over the human throng!
You, who dared in the dark eclipse,—
  When the pygmy heir of a giant name
  Dimmed the face of the land with shame,—
Speak the truth with indignant lips,
Call him little whom men called great,
    Scoff at him, scorn him, deny him,
Point to the blood on his robe of state,
    Fling back his bribes and defy him!

You, who fronted the waves of fate
  As you faced the sea from your island home,
Exiled, yet with a soul elate,
  Sending songs o'er the rolling foam,
Bidding the heart of man to wait
    For the day when all should see

IN PRAISE OF POETS

Floods of wrath from the frowning skies
Fall on an Empire founded in lies,
And France again be free!
You, who came in the Terrible Year
Swiftly back to your broken land,
Now to your heart a thousand times more dear,—
Prayed for her, sung to her, fought for her,
Patiently, fervently wrought for her,
Till once again,
After the storm of fear and pain,
High in the heavens the star of France stood clear!

You, who knew that a man must take
Good and ill with a steadfast soul,
Holding fast, while the billows roll
Over his head, to the things that make
Life worth living for great and small,
Honour and pity and truth,
The heart and the hope of youth,
And the good God over all!
You, to whom work was rest,
Dauntless Toiler of the Sea,
Following ever the joyful quest
Of beauty on the shores of old Romance,
Bard of the poor of France,
And warrior-priest of world-wide charity!
You who loved little children best
Of all the poets that ever sung,

VICTOR HUGO

Great heart, golden heart,
Old, and yet ever young,
Minstrel of liberty,
Lover of all free, winged things,
Now at last you are free,—
Your soul has its wings!
Heart of France for a hundred years,
Floating far in the light that never fails you,
Over the turmoil of mortal hopes and fears
Victor, forever victor, the whole world hails you!

March, 1902.

LONGFELLOW

In a great land, a new land, a land full of labour and
riches and confusion,
Where there were many running to and fro, and shouting, and striving together,
In the midst of the hurry and the troubled noise, I heard
the voice of one singing.

"What are you doing there, O man, singing quietly amid
all this tumult?
This is the time for new inventions, mighty shoutings,
and blowings of the trumpet."
But he answered, "I am only shepherding my sheep
with music."

So he went along his chosen way, keeping his little flock
around him;
And he paused to listen, now and then, beside the antique fountains,
Where the faces of forgotten gods were refreshed with
musically falling waters;

Or he sat for a while at the blacksmith's door, and heard
the cling-clang of the anvils;
Or he rested beneath old steeples full of bells, that
showered their chimes upon him;
Or he walked along the border of the sea, drinking in
the long roar of the billows;

Or he sunned himself in the pine-scented shipyard, amid
the tattoo of the mallets;
Or he leaned on the rail of the bridge, letting his thoughts
flow with the whispering river;
He hearkened also to ancient tales, and made them
young again with his singing.

Then a flaming arrow of death fell on his flock, and
pierced the heart of his dearest!
Silent the music now, as the shepherd entered the
mystical temple of sorrow:
Long he tarried in darkness there: but when he came
out he was singing.

And I saw the faces of men and women and children
silently turning toward him;
The youth setting out on the journey of life, and the old
man waiting beside the last mile-stone;
The toiler sweating beneath his load; and the happy
mother rocking her cradle;

The lonely sailor on far-off seas; and the gray-minded
scholar in his book-room;
The mill-hand bound to a clacking machine; and the
hunter in the forest;
And the solitary soul hiding friendless in the wilderness
of the city;

IN PRAISE OF POETS

Many human faces, full of care and longing, were drawn
irresistibly toward him,
By the charm of something known to every heart, yet
very strange and lovely,
And at the sound of his singing wonderfully all their
faces were lightened.

"Why do you listen, O you people, to this old and world-
worn music?
This is not for you, in the splendour of a new age, in the
democratic triumph!
Listen to the clashing cymbals, the big drums, the brazen
trumpets of your poets."

But the people made no answer, following in their hearts
the simpler music:
For it seemed to them, noise-weary, nothing could be
better worth the hearing
Than the melodies which brought sweet order into life's
confusion.

So the shepherd sang his way along, until he came unto
a mountain:
And I know not surely whether the mountain was called
Parnassus,
But he climbed it out of sight, and still I heard the
voice of one singing.

January, 1907.

THOMAS BAILEY ALDRICH

I

BIRTHDAY VERSES, 1906

DEAR Aldrich, now November's mellow days
  Have brought another *Festa* round to you,
You can't refuse a loving-cup of praise
  From friends the fleeting years have bound to you.

Here come your Marjorie Daw, your dear Bad Boy,
  Prudence, and Judith the Bethulian,
And many more, to wish you birthday joy,
  And sunny hours, and sky cerulean!

Your children all, they hurry to your den,
  With wreaths of honour they have won for you,
To merry-make your threescore years and ten.
  You, old? Why, life has just begun for you!

There's many a reader whom your silver songs
  And crystal stories cheer in loneliness.
What though the newer writers come in throngs?
  You're sure to keep your charm of only-ness.

IN PRAISE OF POETS

You do your work with careful, loving touch,—
  An artist to the very core of you,—
You know the magic spell of "not-too-much":
  We read,—and wish that there was more of you.

And more there is: for while we love your books
  Because their subtle skill is part of you;
We love *you* better, for our friendship looks
  Behind them to the human heart of you.

II

MEMORIAL SONNET, 1908

This is the house where little Aldrich read
  The early pages of Life's wonder-book
  With boyish pleasure: in this ingle-nook
He watched the drift-wood fire of Fancy shed
Bright colour on the pictures blue and red:
  Boy-like he skipped the longer words, and took
  His happy way, with searching, dreamful look
Among the deeper things more simply said.

Then, came his turn to write: and still the flame
  Of Fancy played through all the tales he told,
And still he won the laurelled poet's fame
  With simple words wrought into rhymes of gold.
Look, here's the face to which this house is frame,—
  A man too wise to let his heart grow old!

EDMUND CLARENCE STEDMAN

(Read at His Funeral, January 21, 1908)

OH, quick to feel the lightest touch
  Of beauty or of truth,
Rich in the thoughtfulness of age,
  The hopefulness of youth,
The courage of the gentle heart,
  The wisdom of the pure,
The strength of finely tempered souls
  To labour and endure!

The blue of springtime in your eyes
  Was never quenched by pain;
And winter brought your head the crown
  Of snow without a stain.
The poet's mind, the prince's heart,
  You kept until the end,
Nor ever faltered in your work,
  Nor ever failed a friend.

IN PRAISE OF POETS

You followed, through the quest of life,
  The light that shines above
The tumult and the toil of men,
  And shows us what to love.
Right loyal to the best you knew,
  Reality or dream,
You ran the race, you fought the fight,
  A follower of the Gleam.

We lay upon your folded hands
  The wreath of asphodel;
We speak above your peaceful face
  The tender word *Farewell!*
For well you fare, in God's good care,
  Somewhere within the blue,
And know, to-day, your dearest dreams
  Are true,—and true,—and true!

TO JAMES WHITCOMB RILEY

ON HIS "BOOK OF JOYOUS CHILDREN"

YOURS is a garden of old-fashioned flowers;
  Joyous children delight to play there;
Weary men find rest in its bowers,
  Watching the lingering light of day there.

Old-time tunes and young love-laughter
  Ripple and run among the roses;
Memory's echoes, murmuring after,
  Fill the dusk when the long day closes.

Simple songs with a cadence olden—
  These you learned in the Forest of Arden:
Friendly flowers with hearts all golden—
  These you borrowed from Eden's garden.

This is the reason why all men love you;
  Truth to life is the finest art:
Other poets may soar above you—
  You keep close to the human heart.

December, 1903.

RICHARD WATSON GILDER

IN MEMORIAM

Soul of a soldier in a poet's frame,
Heart of a hero in a body frail;
Thine was the courage clear that did not quail
Before the giant champions of shame
Who wrought dishonour to the city's name;
And thine the vision of the Holy Grail
Of Love, revealed through Music's lucid veil,
Filling thy life with heavenly song and flame.

Pure was the light that lit thy glowing eye,
And strong the faith that held thy simple creed.
Ah, poet, patriot, friend, to serve our need
Thou leavest two great gifts that will not die:
Above the city's noise, thy lyric cry,—
Amid the city's strife, thy noble deed

November, 1909.

THE VALLEY OF VAIN VERSES

The grief that is but feigning,
And weeps melodious tears
Of delicate complaining
From self-indulgent years;
The mirth that is but madness,
And has no inward gladness
Beneath its laughter straining,
To capture thoughtless ears;

The love that is but passion
Of amber-scented lust;
The doubt that is but fashion;
The faith that has no trust;
These Thamyris disperses,
In the Valley of Vain Verses
Below the Mount Parnassian,—
And they crumble into dust.

MUSIC

MUSIC

I

PRELUDE

1

DAUGHTER of Psyche, pledge of that wild night
When, pierced with pain and bitter-sweet delight,
She knew her Love and saw her Lord depart,
Then breathed her wonder and her woe forlorn
Into a single cry, and thou wast born!
Thou flower of rapture and thou fruit of grief;
Invisible enchantress of the heart;
  Mistress of charms that bring relief
  To sorrow, and to joy impart
A heavenly tone that keeps it undefiled,—
    Thou art the child
  Of Amor, and by right divine
    A throne of love is thine,
Thou flower-folded, golden-girdled, star-crowned Queen,
Whose bridal beauty mortal eyes have never seen!

2

Thou art the Angel of the pool that sleeps,
While peace and joy lie hidden in its deeps,
Waiting thy touch to make the waters roll
In healing murmurs round the weary soul.

MUSIC

Ah, when wilt thou draw near,
Thou messenger of mercy robed in song?
My lonely heart has listened for thee long;
And now I seem to hear
Across the crowded market-place of life,
Thy measured foot-fall, ringing light and clear
Above unmeaning noises and unruly strife.
In quiet cadence, sweet and slow,
Serenely pacing to and fro,
Thy far-off steps are magical and dear,—
Ah, turn this way, come close and speak to me!
From this dull bed of languor set my spirit free,
And bid me rise, and let me walk awhile with thee.

II

INVOCATION

Where wilt thou lead me first?
In what still region
Of thy domain,
Whose provinces are legion,
Wilt thou restore me to myself again,
And quench my heart's long thirst?
I pray thee lay thy golden girdle down,
And put away thy starry crown:
For one dear restful hour
Assume a state more mild.
Clad only in thy blossom-broidered gown

That breathes familiar scent of many a flower,
Take the low path that leads through pastures green;
        And though thou art a Queen,
Be Rosamund awhile, and in thy bower,
By tranquil love and simple joy beguiled,
Sing to my soul, as mother to her child.

III

PLAY SONG

  O lead me by the hand,
  And let my heart have rest,
And bring me back to childhood land,
To find again the long-lost band
  Of playmates blithe and blest.

  Some quaint, old-fashioned air,
  That all the children knew,
Shall run before us everywhere,
Like a little maid with flying hair,
  To guide the merry crew.

  Along the garden ways
  We chase the light-foot tune,
And in and out the flowery maze,
With eager haste and fond delays,
  In pleasant paths of June.

For us the fields are new,
For us the woods are rife
With fairy secrets, deep and true,
And heaven is but a tent of blue
Above the game of life.

The world is far away:
The fever and the fret,
And all that makes the heart grow gray,
Is out of sight and far away,
Dear Music, while I hear thee play
That olden, golden roundelay,
"Remember and forget!"

IV

SLEEP SONG

Forget, forget!
The tide of life is turning;
The waves of light ebb slowly down the west:
Along the edge of dark some stars are burning
To guide thy spirit safely to an isle of rest.
A little rocking on the tranquil deep
Of song, to soothe thy yearning,
A little slumber and a little sleep,
And so, forget, forget!

MUSIC

Forget, forget,—
The day was long in pleasure;
Its echoes die away across the hill;
Now let thy heart beat time to their slow measure,
That swells, and sinks, and faints, and falls, till all is still.
Then, like a weary child that loves to keep
Locked in its arms some treasure,
Thy soul in calm content shall fall asleep,
And so forget, forget.

Forget, forget,—
And if thou hast been weeping,
Let go the thoughts that bind thee to thy grief:
Lie still, and watch the singing angels, reaping
The golden harvest of thy sorrow, sheaf by sheaf;
Or count thy joys like flocks of snow-white sheep
That one by one come creeping
Into the quiet fold, until thou sleep,
And so forget, forget!

Forget, forget,—
Thou art a child and knowest
So little of thy life! But music tells
The secret of the world through which thou goest
To work with morning song, to rest with evening bells:
Life is in tune with harmony so deep
That when the notes are lowest
Thou still canst lay thee down in peace and sleep,
For God will not forget.

V

HUNTING SONG

Out of the garden of playtime, out of the bower of rest,
Fain would I follow at daytime, music that calls to a quest.
Hark, how the galloping measure
Quickens the pulses of pleasure;
Gaily saluting the morn
With the long, clear note of the hunting-horn,
Echoing up from the valley,
Over the mountain side,—
Rally, you hunters, rally,
Rally, and ride!

Drink of the magical potion music has mixed with her wine,
Full of the madness of motion, joyful, exultant, divine!
Leave all your troubles behind you,
Ride where they never can find you,
Into the gladness of morn,
With the long, clear note of the hunting-horn,
Swiftly o'er hillock and hollow,
Sweeping along with the wind,—
Follow, you hunters, follow,
Follow and find!

What will you reach with your riding? What is the charm of the chase?
Just the delight and the striding swing of the jubilant pace.

Danger is sweet when you front her,—
In at the death, every hunter!
Now on the breeze the mort is borne
In the long, clear note of the hunting-horn,
Winding merrily, over and over,—
Come, come, come!
Home again, Ranger! home again, Rover!
Turn again, home!

VI

DANCE-MUSIC

1

Now let the sleep-tune blend with the play-tune,
Weaving the mystical spell of the dance;
Lighten the deep tune, soften the gay tune,
Mingle a tempo that turns in a trance.
Half of it sighing, half of it smiling,
Smoothly it swings, with a triplicate beat;
Calling, replying, yearning, beguiling,
Wooing the heart and bewitching the feet.
Every drop of blood
Rises with the flood,
Rocking on the waves of the strain;
Youth and beauty glide
Turning with the tide—
Music making one out of twain,

Bearing them away, and away, and away,
Like a tone and its terce—
Till the chord dissolves, and the dancers stay,
And reverse.

Violins leading, take up the measure,
Turn with the tune again,—clarinets clear
Answer their pleading,—harps full of pleasure
Sprinkle their silver like light on the mere.
Semiquaver notes,
Merry little motes,
Tangled in the haze
Of the lamp's golden rays,
Quiver everywhere
In the air,
Like a spray,—
Till the fuller stream of the might of the tune,
Gliding like a dream in the light of the moon,
Bears them all away, and away, and away,
Floating in the trance of the dance.

2

Then begins a measure stately,
Languid, slow, serene;
All the dancers move sedately,
Stepping leisurely and straitly,
With a courtly mien;

Crossing hands and changing places,
Bowing low between,
While the minuet inlaces
Waving arms and woven paces,—
Glittering damaskeen.
Where is she whose form is folden
In its royal sheen?
From our longing eyes withholden
By her mystic girdle golden,
Beauty sought but never seen,
Music walks the maze, a queen.

VII

WAR-MUSIC

Break off! Dance no more!
Danger is at the door.
Music is in arms.
To signal war's alarms.

Hark, a sudden trumpet calling
Over the hill!
Why are you calling, trumpet, calling?
What is your will?

Men, men, men!
Men who are ready to fight
For their country's life, and the right

MUSIC

Of a liberty-loving land to be
  Free, free, free!
Free from a tyrant's chain,
Free from dishonor's stain,
Free to guard and maintain
All that her fathers fought for,
All that her sons have wrought for,
  Resolute, brave, and free!

  Call again, trumpet, call again,
    Call up the men!

Do you hear the storm of cheers
Mingled with the women's tears
And the tramp, tramp, tramp of marching feet?
Do you hear the throbbing drum
As the hosts of battle come
Keeping time, time, time to its beat?
O Music give a song
To make their spirit strong
For the fury of the tempest they must meet.

  The hoarse roar
  Of the monster guns;
  And the sharp bark
  Of the lesser guns;
  The whine of the shells,
  The rifles' clatter

MUSIC

Where the bullets patter,
The rattle, rattle, rattle
Of the mitrailleuse in battle,
And the yells
Of the men who charge through hells
Where the poison gas descends,
And the bursting shrapnel rends
Limb from limb
In the dim
Chaos and clamor of the strife
Where no man thinks of his life
But only of fighting through,
Blindly fighting through, through!

'Tis done
At last!
The victory won,
The dissonance of warfare past!

O Music mourn the dead
Whose loyal blood was shed,
And sound the taps for every hero slain;
Then lead into the song
That made their spirit strong,
And tell the world they did not die in vain.

Thank God we can see, in the glory of morn,
The invincible flag that our fathers defended;

And our hearts can repeat what the heroes have sworn,
That war shall not end till the war-lust is ended.
Then the bloodthirsty sword shall no longer be lord
Of the nations oppressed by the conqueror's horde,
But the banners of Liberty proudly shall wave
O'er the *world* of the free and the lands of the brave.

May, 1916.

VIII

THE SYMPHONY

Music, they do thee wrong who say thine art
Is only to enchant the sense.
For every timid motion of the heart,
And every passion too intense
To bear the chain of the imperfect word,
And every tremulous longing, stirred
By spirit winds that come we know not whence
And go we know not where,
And every inarticulate prayer
Beating about the depths of pain or bliss,
Like some bewildered bird
That seeks its nest but knows not where it is,
And every dream that haunts, with dim delight,
The drowsy hour between the day and night,
The wakeful hour between the night and day,—
Imprisoned, waits for thee,
Impatient, yearns for thee,

MUSIC

The queen who comes to set the captive free!
Thou lendest wings to grief to fly away,
And wings to joy to reach a heavenly height;
And every dumb desire that storms within the breast
Thou leadest forth to sob or sing itself to rest.

All these are thine, and therefore love is thine.
For love is joy and grief,
And trembling doubt, and certain-sure belief,
And fear, and hope, and longing unexpressed,
In pain most human, and in rapture brief
Almost divine.
Love would possess, yet deepens when denied;
And love would give, yet hungers to receive;
Love like a prince his triumph would achieve;
And like a miser in the dark his joys would hide.
Love is most bold,
He leads his dreams like armèd men in line;
Yet when the siege is set, and he must speak,
Calling the fortress to resign
Its treasure, valiant love grows weak,
And hardly dares his purpose to unfold.
Less with his faltering lips than with his eyes
He claims the longed-for prize:
Love fain would tell it all, yet leaves the best untold.
But thou shalt speak for love. Yea, thou shalt teach
The mystery of measured tone,
The Pentecostal speech

That every listener heareth as his own.
For on thy head the cloven tongues of fire,—
Diminished chords that quiver with desire,
And major chords that glow with perfect peace,—
    Have fallen from above;
    And thou canst give release
In music to the burdened heart of love.

Sound with the 'cellos' pleading, passionate strain
The yearning theme, and let the flute reply
In placid melody, while violins complain,
        And sob, and sigh,
        With muted string;
  Then let the oboe half-reluctant sing
  Of bliss that trembles on the verge of pain,
    While 'cellos plead and plead again,
With throbbing notes delayed, that would impart
To every urgent tone the beating of the heart.
    So runs the andante, making plain
The hopes and fears of love without a word.
Then comes the adagio, with a yielding theme
Through which the violas flow soft as in a dream,
    While horns and mild bassoons are heard
    In tender tune, that seems to float
        Like an enchanted boat
    Upon the downward-gliding stream,
    Toward the allegro's wide, bright sea
    Of dancing, glittering, blending tone,

Where every instrument is sounding free,
And harps like wedding-chimes are rung, and trumpets blown
Around the barque of love
That rides, with smiling skies above,
A royal galley, many-oared,
Into the happy harbour of the perfect chord.

IX

IRIS

Light to the eye and Music to the ear,—
These are the builders of the bridge that springs
From earth's dim shore of half-remembered things
To reach the heavenly sphere
Where nothing silent is and nothing dark.
So when I see the rainbow's arc
Spanning the showery sky, far-off I hear
Music, and every colour sings:
And while the symphony builds up its round
Full sweep of architectural harmony
Above the tide of Time, far, far away I see
A bow of colour in the bow of sound.
Red as the dawn the trumpet rings;
Blue as the sky, the choir of strings
Darkens in double-bass to ocean's hue,
Rises in violins to noon-tide's blue,
With threads of quivering light shot through and through;

MUSIC

Green as the mantle that the summer flings
Around the world, the pastoral reeds in tune
Embroider melodies of May and June.
Purer than gold,
Yea, thrice-refinèd gold,
And richer than the treasures of the mine,
Floods of the human voice divine
Along the arch in choral song are rolled.
So bends the bow complete:
And radiant rapture flows
Across the bridge, so full, so strong, so sweet,
That the uplifted spirit hardly knows
Whether the Music-Light that glows
Within the arch of tones and colours seven,
Is sunset-peace of earth or sunrise-joy of Heaven.

X

SEA AND SHORE

Music, I yield to thee
As swimmer to the sea,
I give my spirit to the flood of song!
Bear me upon thy breast
In rapture and at rest,
Bathe me in pure delight and make me strong;
From strife and struggle bring release,
And draw the waves of passion into tides of peace.

MUSIC

Remembered songs most dear
In living songs I hear,
While blending voices gently swing and sway,
In melodies of love,
Whose mighty currents move
With singing near and singing far away;
Sweet in the glow of morning light,
And sweeter still across the starlit gulf of night.

Music, in thee we float,
And lose the lonely note
Of self in thy celestial-ordered strain,
Until at last we find
The life to love resigned
In harmony of joy restored again;
And songs that cheered our mortal days
Break on the shore of light in endless hymns of praise.

December, 1901—May, 1903—May, 1916.

MASTER OF MUSIC

(In memory of Theodore Thomas, 1905)

GLORY of architect, glory of painter, and sculptor, and bard,
Living forever in temple and picture and statue and song,—
Look how the world with the lights that they lit is illumined and starred;
Brief was the flame of their life, but the lamps of their art burn long!

Where is the Master of Music, and how has he vanished away?
Where is the work that he wrought with his wonderful art in the air?
Gone,—it is gone like the glow on the cloud at the close of the day!
The Master has finished his work and the glory of music is—where?

MASTER OF MUSIC

Once, at the wave of his wand, all the billows of musical sound
Followed his will, as the sea was ruled by the prophet of old:
Now that his hand is relaxed, and his rod has dropped to the ground,
Silent and dark are the shores where the marvellous harmonies rolled!

Nay, but not silent the hearts that were filled by that life-giving sea;
Deeper and purer forever the tides of their being will roll,
Grateful and joyful, O Master, because they have listened to thee;
The glory of music endures in the depths of the human soul.

THE PIPES O' PAN

GREAT Nature had a million words,
In tongues of trees and songs of birds,
But none to breathe the heart of man,
Till Music filled the pipes o' Pan.

1909.

TO A YOUNG GIRL SINGING

Oh, what do you know of the song, my dear,
And how have you made it your own?
You have caught the turn of the melody clear,
And you give it again with a golden tone,
Till the wonder-word and the wedded note
Are flowing out of your beautiful throat
With a liquid charm for every ear:
And they talk of your art,—but for you alone
The song is a thing, unheard, unknown;
You only have learned it by rote.

But when you have lived for awhile, my dear,
I think you will learn it anew!
For a joy will come, or a grief, or a fear,
That will alter the look of the world for you;
And the lyric you learned as a bit of art,
Will wake to life as a wonderful part
Of the love you feel so deep and true;
And the thrill of a laugh or the throb of a tear,
Will come with your song to all who hear;
For then you will know it by heart.

April, 1911.

THE OLD FLUTE

The time will come when I no more can play
This polished flute: the stops will not obey
My gnarled fingers; and the air it weaves
In modulations, like a vine with leaves
Climbing around the tower of song, will die
In rustling autumn rhythms, confused and dry.
My shortened breath no more will freely fill
This magic reed with melody at will;
My stiffened lips will try and try in vain
To wake the liquid, leaping, dancing strain;
The heavy notes will falter, wheeze, and faint,
Or mock my ear with shrillness of complaint.

Then let me hang this faithful friend of mine
Upon the trunk of some old, sacred pine,
And sit beneath the green protecting boughs
To hear the viewless wind, that sings and soughs
Above me, play its wild, aerial lute,
And draw a ghost of music from my flute!

So will I thank the gods; and most of all
The Delian Apollo, whom men call
The mighty master of immortal sound,—
Lord of the billows in their chanting round,
Lord of the winds that fill the wood with sighs,

THE OLD FLUTE

Lord of the echoes and their sweet replies,
Lord of the little people of the air
That sprinkle drops of music everywhere,
Lord of the sea of melody that laves
The universe with never silent waves,—
Him will I thank that this brief breath of mine
Has caught one cadence of the song divine;
And these frail fingers learned to rise and fall
In time with that great tune which throbs thro' all;
And these poor lips have lent a lilt of joy
To songless men whom weary tasks employ!
My life has had its music, and my heart
In harmony has borne a little part,
And now I come with quiet, grateful breast
To Death's dim hall of silence and of rest.

Freely rendered from the French of Auguste Angellier, 1911.

THE FIRST BIRD O' SPRING

TO OLIVE WHEELER

WINTER on Mount Shasta,
April down below;
Golden hours of glowing sun,
Sudden showers of snow!
Under leafless thickets
Early wild-flowers cling;
But, oh, my dear, I'm fain to hear
The first bird o' Spring!

Alders are in tassel,
Maples are in bud;
Waters of the blue McCloud
Shout in joyful flood;
Through the giant pine-trees
Flutters many a wing;
But, oh, my dear, I long to hear
The first bird o' Spring!

THE FIRST BIRD O' SPRING

Candle-light and fire-light
Mingle at "the Bend;"
'Neath the roof of Bo-hai-pan
Light and shadow blend.
Sweeter than a wood-thrush
A maid begins to sing;
And, oh, my dear, I'm glad to hear
The first bird o' Spring!

The Bend, California, April 29, 1913.

THE HOUSE OF RIMMON

A DRAMA IN FOUR ACTS

DRAMATIS PERSONÆ

BENHADAD:	King of Damascus.
REZON:	High Priest of the House of Rimmon.
SABALLIDIN:	A Noble.
HAZAEL IZDUBHAR RAKHAZ	Courtiers.
SHUMAKIM:	The King's Fool.
ELISHA:	Prophet of Israel.
NAAMAN:	Captain of the Armies of Damascus.
RUAHMAH:	A Captive Maid of Israel.
TSARPI:	Wife to Naaman.
KHAMMA NUBTA	Attendants of Tsarpi.

Soldiers, Servants, Citizens, etc., etc.

SCENE: *Damascus and the Mountains of Samaria.*

TIME: 850 *B. C.*

ACT I

Scene I

Night, in the garden of Naaman *at Damascus. At the left the palace, with softly gleaming lights and music coming from the open latticed windows. The garden is full of oleanders, roses, pomegranates, abundance of crimson flowers; the air is heavy with their fragrance: a fountain at the right is plashing gently: behind it is an arbour covered with vines. Near the centre of the garden stands a small, hideous image of the god Rimmon. Beyond the arbour rises the lofty square tower of the House of Rimmon, which casts a shadow from the moon across the garden. The background is a wide, hilly landscape, with the snow-clad summit of Mount Hermon in the distance. Enter by the palace door, the lady* Tsarpi, *robed in red and gold, and followed by her maids,* Khamma *and* Nubta. *She remains on the terrace: they go down into the garden, looking about, and returning to her.*

Khamma:

There's no one here; the garden is asleep.

Nubta:

The flowers are nodding, all the birds abed,—
Nothing awake except the watchful stars!

Khamma:

The stars are sentinels discreet and mute:
How many things they know and never tell!

TSARPI: [*Impatiently.*]
Unlike the stars, how many things you tell
And do not know! When comes your master home?

NUBTA:
Lady, his armour-bearer brought us word,—
At moonset, not before.

TSARPI:
He haunts the camp
And leaves me much alone; yet I can pass
The time of absence not unhappily,
If I but know the time of his return.
An hour of moonlight yet! Khamma, my mirror!
These curls are ill arranged, this veil too low,—
So,—that is better, careless maids! Withdraw,—
But bring me word if Naaman appears!

KHAMMA:
Mistress, have no concern; for when we hear
The clatter of his horse along the street,
We'll run this way and lead your dancers down
With song and laughter,—you shall know in time.

[*Exeunt* KHAMMA *and* NUBTA *laughing,* TSARPI *descends the steps.*]

TSARPI:
My guest is late; but he will surely come!
The man who burns to drain the cup of love,
The priest whose greed of glory never fails,
Both, both have need of me, and he will come.
And I,—what do I need? Why everything

That helps my beauty to a higher throne;
All that a priest can promise, all a man
Can give, and all a god bestow, I need:
This may a woman win, and this will I.

[*Enter* REZON *quietly from the shadow of the trees. He stands behind* TSARPI *and listens, smiling, to her last words. Then he drops his mantle of leopard-skin, and lifts his high priest's rod of bronze, shaped at one end like a star.*]

REZON:

Tsarpi!

TSARPI: [*Bowing low before him.*]

The mistress of the house of Naaman
Salutes the master of the House of Rimmon.

REZON:

Rimmon receives you with his star of peace,
For you were once a handmaid of his altar.

[*He lowers the star-point of the rod, which glows for a moment with rosy light above her head.*]

And now the keeper of his temple asks
The welcome of the woman for the man.

TSARPI: [*Giving him her hand, but holding off his embrace.*]

No more,—till I have heard what brings you here
By night, within the garden of the one
Who scorns you most and fears you least in all
Damascus.

REZON:

Trust me, I repay his scorn

With double hatred,—Naaman, the man
Who stands against the nobles and the priests,
This powerful fool, this impious devotee
Of liberty, who loves the people more
Than he reveres the city's ancient god:
This frigid husband who sets you below
His dream of duty to a horde of slaves:
This man I hate, and I will humble him.

TSARPI:

I think I hate him too. He stands apart
From me, ev'n while he holds me in his arms,
By something that I cannot understand.
He swears he loves his wife next to his honour!
Next? That's too low! I will be first or nothing.

REZON:

With me you are the first, the absolute!
When you and I have triumphed you shall reign;
And you and I will bring this hero down.

TSARPI:

But how? For he is strong.

REZON:

By this, the hand
Of Tsarpi; and by this, the rod of Rimmon.

TSARPI:

Your plan?

REZON:

You know the host of Nineveh
Is marching now against us. Envoys come

To bid us yield before a hopeless war.
Our king is weak: the nobles, being rich,
Would purchase peace to make them richer still:
Only the people and the soldiers, led
By Naaman, would fight for liberty.
Blind fools! To-day the envoys came to me,
And talked with me in secret. Promises,
Great promises! For every noble house
That urges peace, a noble recompense:
The King, submissive, kept in royal state
And splendour: most of all, honour and wealth
Shall crown the House of Rimmon, and his priest,—
Yea, and his priestess! For we two will rise
Upon the city's fall. The common folk
Shall suffer; Naaman shall sink with them
In wreck; but I shall rise, and you shall rise
Above me! You shall climb, through incense-smoke,
And days of pomp, and nights of revelry,
Unto the topmost room in Rimmon's tower,
The secret, lofty room, the couch of bliss,
And the divine embraces of the god.

TSARPI: [*Throwing out her arms in exultation.*]
All, all I wish! What must I do for this?

REZON:
Turn Naaman away from thoughts of war.

TSARPI:
But if I fail? His will is proof against
The lure of kisses and the wile of tears.

REZON:

Where woman fails, woman and priest succeed.
Before the King decides, he must consult
The oracle of Rimmon. This my hands
Prepare,—and you shall read the signs prepared
In words of fear to melt the brazen heart
Of Naaman.

TSARPI:

But if it flame instead?

REZON:

I know a way to quench that flame. The cup,
The parting cup your hand shall give to him!
What if the curse of Rimmon should infect
That sacred wine with poison, secretly
To work within his veins, week after week
Corrupting all the currents of his blood,
Dimming his eyes, wasting his flesh? What then?
Would he prevail in war? Would he come back
To glory, or to shame? What think you?

TSARPI:

I?—
I do not think; I only do my part.
But can the gods bless this?

REZON:

The gods can bless
Whatever they decree; their will makes right;
And this is for the glory of the House

Of Rimmon,—and for thee, my queen. Come, come!
The night grows dark: we'll perfect our alliance.

[REZON *draws her with him, embracing her, through the shadows of the garden.* RUAHMAH, *who has been sleeping in the arbour, has been awakened during the dialogue, and has been dimly visible in her white dress, behind the vines. She parts them and comes out, pushing back her long, dark hair from her temples.*]

RUAHMAH:

What have I heard? O God, what shame is this
Plotted beneath Thy pure and silent stars!
Was it for this that I was brought away
A captive from the hills of Israel
To serve the heathen in a land of lies?
Ah, treacherous, shameful priest! Ah, shameless wife
Of one too noble to suspect thy guilt!
The very greatness of his generous heart
Betrays him to their hands. What can I do!
Nothing,—a slave,—hated and mocked by all
My fellow-slaves! O bitter prison-life!
I smother in this black, betraying air
Of lust and luxury; I faint beneath
The shadow of this House of Rimmon. God
Have mercy! Lead me out to Israel.
To Israel!

[*Music and laughter heard within the palace. The doors fly open and a flood of men and women, dancers, players, flushed with wine, dishevelled, pour down the steps,* KHAMMA *and* NUBTA *with them. They crown the image with roses and dance around it.* RUAHMAH *is discovered crouching beside the arbour. They drag her out beside the image.*]

NUBTA:

Look! Here's the Hebrew maid,—
She's homesick; let us comfort her!

KHAMMA: [*They put their arms around her.*]
Yes, dancing is the cure for homesickness.
We'll make her dance.

RUAHMAH: [*She slips away.*]
I pray you, let me go!
I cannot dance, I do not know your measures.

KHAMMA:
Then sing for us,—a song of Israel!

RUAHMAH:
How can I sing the songs of Israel
In this strange country? O my heart would break!

A SERVANT:
A stubborn and unfriendly maid! We'll whip her.
[*They circle around her, striking her with rose-branches; she sinks to her knees, covering her face with her bare arms, which bleed.*]

NUBTA:
Look, look! She kneels to Rimmon, she is tamed.

RUAHMAH: [*Springing up and lifting her arms.*]
Nay, not to this dumb idol, but to Him
Who made Orion and the seven stars!

ALL:
She raves,—she mocks at Rimmon! Punish her!
The fountain! Wash her blasphemy away!
[*They push her toward the fountain, laughing and shouting. In the open door of the palace* NAAMAN *appears, dressed in blue and silver, bareheaded and unarmed. He comes to the top of the steps and stands for a moment, astonished and angry.*]

NAAMAN:
Silence! What drunken rout is this? Begone,
Ye barking dogs and mewing cats! Out, all!
Poor child, what have they done to thee?
[*Exeunt all except* RUAHMAH, *who stands with her face covered by her hands.* NAAMAN *comes to her, laying his hand on her shoulder.*]

RUAHMAH: [*Looking up in his face.*]
Nothing,
My lord and master! They have harmed me not.

NAAMAN: [*Touching her arm.*]
Dost call this nothing?

RUAHMAH:
Since my lord is come!

NAAMAN:
I do not know thy face,—who art thou, child?

RUAHMAH:

The handmaid of thy wife.

NAAMAN:

Whence comest thou?

Thy voice is like thy mistress, but thy looks
Have something foreign. Tell thy name, thy land.

RUAHMAH:

Ruahmah is my name, a captive maid,
The daughter of a prince in Israel,
Where once, in olden days, I saw my lord
Ride through our highlands, when Samaria
Was allied with Damascus to defeat
Our common foe.

NAAMAN:

And thou rememberest this?

RUAHMAH:

As clear as yesterday! Master, I saw
Thee riding on a snow-white horse beside
Our king; and all we joyful little maids
Strewed boughs of palm along the victors' way,
For you had driven out the enemy,
Broken; and both our lands were friends and free.

NAAMAN: [*Sadly.*]

Well, they are past, those noble days! The days
When nations would imperil all to keep
Their liberties, are only memories now.
The common cause is lost,—and thou art brought,
The captive of some mercenary raid,

Some skirmish of a gold-begotten war,
To serve within my house. Dost thou fare well?

RUAHMAH:

Master, thou seest.

NAAMAN:

Yes, I see! My child,
Why do they hate thee so?

RUAHMAH:

I do not know,
Unless because I will not bow to Rimmon.

NAAMAN:

Thou needest not. I fear he is a god
Who pities not his people, will not save.
My heart is sick with doubt of him. But thou
Shalt hold thy faith,—I care not what it is,—
Worship thy god; but keep thy spirit free.

[*He takes the amulet from his neck and gives it to her.*]

Here, take this chain and wear it with my seal,
None shall molest the maid who carries this.
Thou hast found favour in thy master's eyes;
Hast thou no other gift to ask of me?

RUAHMAH: [*Earnestly.*]

My lord, I do entreat thee not to go
To-morrow to the council. Seek the King
And speak with him in secret; but avoid
The audience-hall.

NAAMAN:

Why, what is this? Thy wits
Are wandering. My honour is engaged
To speak for war, to lead in war against
The Assyrian Bull and save Damascus.

RUAHMAH: [*With confused earnestness.*]
Then, lord, if thou must go, I pray thee speak,—
I know not how,—but so that all must hear.
With magic of unanswerable words
Persuade thy foes. Yet watch,—beware,—

NAAMAN:

Of what?

RUAHMAH: [*Turning aside.*]
I am entangled in my speech,—no light,—
How shall I tell him? He will not believe.
O my dear lord, thine enemies are they
Of thine own house. I pray thee to beware,—
Beware,—of Rimmon!

NAAMAN:

Child, thy words are wild:
Thy troubles have bewildered all thy brain.
Go, now, and fret no more; but sleep, and dream
Of Israel! For thou shalt see thy home
Among the hills again.

RUAHMAH:

Master, good-night.
And may thy slumber be as sweet and deep
As if thou camped at snowy Hermon's foot,

Amid the music of his waterfalls.
There friendly oak-trees bend their boughs above
The weary head, pillowed on earth's kind breast,
And unpolluted breezes lightly breathe
A song of sleep among the murmuring leaves.
There the big stars draw nearer, and the sun
Looks forth serene, undimmed by city's mirk
Or smoke of idol-temples, to behold
The waking wonder of the wide-spread world.
There life renews itself with every morn
In purest joy of living. May the Lord
Deliver thee, dear master, from the nets
Laid for thy feet, and lead thee out along
The open path, beneath the open sky!

[*Exit* RUAHMAH: NAAMAN *stands looking after her.*]

SCENE II

TIME: *The following morning*

The audience-hall in BENHADAD'S *palace. The sides of the hall are lined with lofty columns: the back opens toward the city, with descending steps: the House of Rimmon with its high tower is seen in the background. The throne is at the right in front: opposite is the royal door of entrance, guarded by four tall sentinels. Enter at the rear between the columns,* RAKHAZ, SABALLIDIN, HAZAEL, IZDUBHAR.

IZDUBHAR: [*An excited old man.*]

The city is all in a turmoil. It boils like a pot of

lentils. The people are foaming and bubbling round and round like beans in the pottage.

HAZAEL: [*A lean, crafty man.*]

Fear is a hot fire.

RAKHAZ: [*A fat, pompous man.*]

Well may they fear, for the Assyrians are not three days distant. They are blazing along like a water-spout to chop Damascus down like a pitcher of spilt milk.

SABALLIDIN: [*Young and frank.*]

Cannot Naaman drive them back?

RAKHAZ: [*Puffing and blowing.*]

Ho! Naaman? Where have you been living? Naaman is a broken reed whose claws have been cut. Build no hopes on that foundation, for it will run away and leave you all adrift in the conflagration.

SABALLIDIN:

He clatters like a windmill. What would he say, Hazael?

HAZAEL:

Naaman can do nothing without the command of the King; and the King fears to order the army to march without the approval of the gods. The High Priest is against it. The House of Rimmon is for peace with Asshur.

RAKHAZ:

Yes, and all the nobles are for peace. We are the

men whose wisdom lights the rudder that upholds the chariot of state. Would we be rich if we were not wise? Do we not know better than the rabble what medicine will silence this fire that threatens to drown us?

IZDUBHAR:

But if the Assyrians come, we shall all perish; they will despoil us all.

HAZAEL:

Not us, my lord, only the common people. The envoys have offered favourable terms to the priests, and the nobles, and the King. No palace, no temple, shall be plundered. Only the shops, and the markets, and the houses of the multitude shall be given up to the Bull. He will eat his supper from the pot of lentils, not from our golden plate.

RAKHAZ:

Yes, and all who speak for peace in the council shall be enriched; our heads shall be crowned with seats of honour in the procession of the Assyrian king. He needs wise counsellors to help him guide the ship of empire onto the solid rock of prosperity. You must be with us, my lords Izdubhar and Saballidin, and let the stars of your wisdom roar loudly for peace.

IZDUBHAR:

He talks like a tablet read upside down,—a wild ass

braying in the wilderness. Yet there is policy in his words.

SABALLIDIN:

I know not. Can a kingdom live without a people or an army? If we let the Bull in to sup on the lentils, will he not make his breakfast in our vineyards?

[*Enter other courtiers following* SHUMAKIM, *a humpbacked jester, in blue, green and red, a wreath of poppies around his neck and a flagon in his hand. He walks unsteadily, and stutters in his speech.*]

HAZAEL:

Here is Shumakim, the King's fool, with his legs full of last night's wine.

SHUMAKIM: [*Balancing himself in front of them and chuckling.*]

Wrong, my lords, very wrong! This is not last night's wine, but a draught the King's physician gave me this morning for a cure. It sobers me amazingly! I know you all, my lords: any fool would know you. You, master, are a statesman; and you are a politician; and you are a patriot.

RAKHAZ:

Am I a statesman? I felt something of the kind about me. But what is a statesman?

SHUMAKIM:

A politician that is stuffed with big words; a fat

man in a mask; one that plays a solemn tune on a sackbut full o' wind.

HAZAEL:

And what is a politician?

SHUMAKIM:

A statesman that has dropped his mask and cracked his sackbut. Men trust him for what he is, and he never deceives them, because he always lies.

IZDUBHAR:

Why do you call me a patriot?

SHUMAKIM:

Because you know what is good for you; you love your country as you love your pelf. You feel for the common people,—as the wolf feels for the sheep.

SABALLIDIN:

And what am I?

SHUMAKIM:

A fool, master, just a plain fool; and there is hope of thee for that reason. Embrace me, brother, and taste this; but not too much,—it will intoxicate thee with sobriety.

[*The hall has been slowly filling with courtiers and soldiers; a crowd of people begin to come up the steps at the rear, where they are halted by a chain guarded by servants of the palace. A bell tolls; the royal door is thrown open; the aged King totters across the hall and takes his seat on the throne with the four tall sentinels standing behind him. All bow down shading their eyes with their hands.*]

BENHADAD:

The hour of royal audience is come.
I'll hear the envoys. Are my counsellors
At hand? Where are the priests of Rimmon's house?

[*Gongs sound.* REZON *comes in from the side, followed by a procession of priests in black and yellow. The courtiers bow; the King rises;* REZON *takes his stand on the steps of the throne at the left of the King.*]

BENHADAD:

Where is my faithful servant Naaman,
The captain of my host?

[*Trumpets sound from the city. The crowd on the steps divide; the chain is lowered;* NAAMAN *enters, followed by six soldiers. He is dressed in chain-mail with a silver helmet and a cloak of blue. He uncovers, and kneels on the steps of the throne at the King's right.*]

NAAMAN:

My lord the King,
The bearer of thy sword is here.

BENHADAD: [*Giving* NAAMAN *his hand, and sitting down.*]

Welcome,
My strong right arm that never me failed yet!
I am in doubt,—but stay thou close to me

While I decide this cause. Where are the envoys?
Let them appear and give their message.

[*Enter the Assyrian envoys; one in white and the other in red; both with the golden Bull's head embroidered on their robes. They come from the right, rear, bow slightly before the throne, and take the centre of the hall.*]

WHITE ENVOY: [*Stepping forward.*]

Greeting from Shalmaneser, Asshur's son,
Who rules the world from Nineveh,
Unto Benhadad, monarch in Damascus!
The conquering Bull has led his army forth;
The south has fallen before him, and the west
His feet have trodden; Hamath is laid waste;
He pauses at your gate, invincible,—
To offer peace. The princes of your court,
The priests of Rimmon's house, and you, the King,
If you pay homage to your Overlord,
Shall rest secure, and flourish as our friends.
Assyria sends to you this gilded yoke;
Receive it as the sign of proffered peace.

[*He lays a yoke on the steps of the throne.*]

BENHADAD:

What of the city? Said your king no word
Of our Damascus, and the many folk
That do inhabit her and make her great?
What of the soldiers who have fought for us?

WHITE ENVOY:

Of these my royal master did not speak.

BENHADAD:

Strange silence! Must we give them up to him?
Is this the price at which he offers us
The yoke of peace? What if we do refuse?

RED ENVOY: [*Stepping forward.*]

Then ruthless war! War to the uttermost.
No quarter, no compassion, no escape!
The Bull will gore and trample in his fury
Nobles and priests and king,—none shall be spared!
Before the throne we lay our second gift;
This bloody horn, the symbol of red war.

[*He lays a long bull's horn, stained with blood, on the steps of the throne.*]

WHITE ENVOY:

Our message is delivered. We return
Unto our master. He will wait three days
To know your royal choice between his gifts.
Keep which you will and send the other back.
The red bull's horn your youngest page may bring;
But with the yoke, best send your mightiest army!

[*The* ENVOYS *retire, amid confused murmurs of the people, the King silent, his head, sunken on his breast.*]

BENHADAD:

Proud words, a bitter message, hard to endure!
We are not now that force which feared no foe:

Our old allies have left us. Can we face the Bull
Alone, and beat him back? Give me your counsel.

[*Many speak at once, confusedly.*]

What babblement is this? Were ye born at Babel?
Give me clear words and reasonable speech.

RAKHAZ: [*Pompously.*]

O King, I am a reasonable man!
And there be some who call me very wise
And prudent; but of this I will not speak,
For I am also modest. Let me plead,
Persuade, and reason you to choose for peace.
This golden yoke may be a bitter draught,
But better far to fold it in our arms,
Than risk our cargoes in the savage horn
Of war. Shall we imperil all our wealth,
Our valuable lives? Nobles are few,
Rich men are rare, and wise men rarer still;
The precious jewels on the tree of life,
Wherein the common people are but bricks
And clay and rubble. Let the city go,
But save the corner-stones that float the ship!
Have I not spoken well?

BENHADAD: [*Shaking his head.*]

Excellent well!

Most eloquent! But misty in the meaning.

HAZAEL: [*With cold decision.*]

Then let me speak, O King, in plainer words!
The days of independent states are past:

The tide of empire sweeps across the earth;
Assyria rides it with resistless power
And thunders on to subjugate the world.
Oppose her, and we fight with Destiny;
Submit to her demands, and we shall ride
With her to victory. Therefore accept
The golden yoke, Assyria's gift of peace.

NAAMAN: [*Starting forward eagerly.*]
There is no peace beneath a conqueror's yoke!
For every state that barters liberty
To win imperial favour, shall be drained
Of her best blood, henceforth, in endless wars
To make the empire greater. Here's the choice,
My King, we fight to keep our country free,
Or else we fight forevermore to help
Assyria bind the world as we are bound.
I am a soldier, and I know the hell
Of war! But I will gladly ride through hell
To save Damascus. Master, bid me ride!
Ten thousand chariots wait for your command;
And twenty thousand horsemen strain the leash
Of patience till you let them go; a throng
Of spearmen, archers, swordsmen, like the sea
Chafing against a dike, roar for the onset!
O master, let me launch your mighty host
Against the Bull,—we'll bring him to his knees!

[*Cries of "war!" from the soldiers and the people; "peace!" from the courtiers and the priests.*

The King rises, turning toward NAAMAN, *and seems about to speak.* REZON *lifts his rod.*]

REZON:

Shall not the gods decide when mortals doubt?
Rimmon is master of the city's fate;
We read his will, by our most ancient-faith,
In omens and in signs of mystery.
Must we not hearken to his high commands?

BENHADAD: [*Sinking back on the throne, submissively.*]

I am the faithful son of Rimmon's House.
Consult the oracle. But who shall read?

REZON:

Tsarpi, the wife of Naaman, who served
Within the temple in her maiden years,
Shall be the mouth-piece of the mighty god,
To-day's high-priestess. Bring the sacrifice!

[*Gongs and cymbals sound: enter priests carrying an altar on which a lamb is bound. The altar is placed in the centre of the hall.* TSARPI *follows the priests, covered with a long transparent veil of black, sown with gold stars;* RUAHMAH, *in white, bears her train.* TSARPI *stands before the altar, facing it, and lifts her right hand holding a knife.* RUAHMAH *steps back, near the throne, her hands crossed on her breast, her head bowed. The priests close in around* TSARPI *and the altar. The knife is seen to strike downward. Gongs and cymbals sound: cries of "Rimmon, hear us!" The circle of priests opens, and* TSARPI *turns slowly to face the King.*]

TSARPI: [*Monotonously.*]

Black is the blood of the victim,
Rimmon is unfavourable,
Asratu is unfavourable;
They will not war against Asshur,
They will make a league with the God of Nineveh.
Evil is in store for Damascus,
A strong enemy will lay waste the land.
Therefore make peace with the Bull;
Hearken to the voice of Rimmon.

[*She turns again to the altar, and the priests close in around her.* REZON *lifts his rod toward the tower of the temple. A flash of lightning followed by thunder; smoke rises from the altar; all except* NAAMAN *and* RUAHMAH *cover their faces. The circle of priests opens again, and* TSARPI *comes forward slowly, chanting.*]

CHANT:

Hear the words of Rimmon! Thus your Maker speaketh:
I, the god of thunder, riding on the whirlwind,
I, the god of lightning leaping from the storm-cloud,
I will smite with vengeance him who dares defy me!
He who leads Damascus into war with Asshur,
Conquering or conquered, bears my curse upon him.

Surely shall my arrow strike his heart in secret,
Burn his flesh with fever, turn his blood to poison,
Brand him with corruption, drive him into darkness;
He shall surely perish by the doom of Rimmon.

[*All are terrified and look toward* NAAMAN, *shuddering.* RUAHMAH *alone seems not to heed the curse, but stands with her eyes fixed on* NAAMAN.]

RUAHMAH:

Be not afraid! There is a greater God
Shall cover thee with His almighty wings:
Beneath his shield and buckler shalt thou trust.

BENHADAD:

Repent, my son, thou must not brave this curse.

NAAMAN:

My King, there is no curse as terrible
As that which lights a bosom-fire for him
Who gives away his honour, to prolong
A craven life whose every breath is shame!
If I betray the men who follow me,
The city that has put her trust in me,
What king can shield me from my own deep scorn
What god release me from that self-made hell?
The tender mercies of Assyria
I know; and they are cruel as creeping tigers.
Give up Damascus, and her streets will run
Rivers of innocent blood; the city's heart,
That mighty, labouring heart, wounded and crushed
Beneath the brutal hooves of the wild Bull,

Will cry against her captain, sitting safe
Among the nobles, in some pleasant place.
I shall be safe,—safe from the threatened wrath
Of unknown gods, but damned forever by
The men I know,—that is the curse I fear.

BENHADAD:

Speak not so high, my son. Must we not bow
Our heads before the sovereignties of heaven?
The unseen rulers are Divine.

NAAMAN:

O King,
I am unlearned in the lore of priests;
Yet well I know that there are hidden powers
About us, working mortal weal and woe
Beyond the force of mortals to control.
And if these powers appear in love and truth,
I think they must be gods, and worship them.
But if their secret will is manifest
In blind decrees of sheer omnipotence,
That punish where no fault is found, and smite
The poor with undeserved calamity,
And pierce the undefended in the dark
With arrows of injustice, and foredoom
The innocent to burn in endless pain,
I will not call this fierce almightiness
Divine. Though I must bear, with every man,
The burden of my life ordained, I'll keep
My soul unterrified, and tread the path

Of truth and honour with a steady heart!
Have ye not heard, my lords? The oracle
Proclaims to me, to me alone, the doom
Of vengeance if I lead the army out.
"Conquered or conquering!" I grip that chance!
Damascus free, her foes all beaten back,
The people saved from slavery, the King
Upheld in honour on his ancient throne,—
O what's the cost of this? I'll gladly pay
Whatever gods there be, whatever price
They ask for this one victory. Give me
This gilded sign of shame to carry back;
I'll shake it in the face of Asshur's king,
And break it on his teeth.

BENHADAD: [*Rising.*]
Then go, my never-beaten captain, go!
And may the powers that hear thy solemn vow
Forgive thy rashness for Damascus' sake,
Prosper thy fighting, and remit thy pledge.

REZON: [*Standing beside the altar.*]
The pledge, O King, this man must seal his pledge
At Rimmon's altar. He must take the cup
Of soldier-sacrament, and bind himself
By thrice-performed libation to abide
The fate he has invoked.

NAAMAN: [*Slowly.*]
And so I will.

[*He comes down the steps, toward the altar, where*

REZON *is filling the cup which* TSARPI *holds.* RUAHMAH *throws herself before* NAAMAN, *clasping his knees.*]

RUAHMAH: [*Passionately and wildly.*]

My lord, I do beseech you, stay! There's death
Within that cup. It is an offering
To devils. See, the wine blazes like fire,
It flows like blood, it is a cursed cup,
Fulfilled of treachery and hate.
Dear master, noble master, touch it not!

NAAMAN:

Poor maid, thy brain is still distraught. Fear not,
But let me go! Here, treat her tenderly!
[*Gives her into the hands of* SABALLIDIN.]
Can harm befall me from the wife who bears
My name? I take the cup of fate from her.
I greet the unknown powers; [*Pours libation.*]
I will perform my vow; [*Again.*]
I will abide my fate; [*Again.*]
I pledge my life to keep Damascus free.
[*He drains the cup, and lets it fall.*]

CURTAIN.

ACT II

TIME: *A week later*

The fore-court of the House of Rimmon. At the back the broad steps and double doors of the shrine; above them the tower of the god, its summit invisible. Enter various groups of citizens, talking, laughing, shouting: RAKHAZ, HAZAEL, SHUMAKIM *and others.*

FIRST CITIZEN:

Great news, glorious news, the Assyrians are beaten!

SECOND CITIZEN:

Naaman is returning, crowned with victory. Glory to our noble captain!

THIRD CITIZEN:

No, he is killed. I had it from one of the camp-followers who saw him fall at the head of the battle. They are bringing his body to bury it with honour. O sorrowful victory!

RAKHAZ:

Peace, my good fellows, you are ignorant, you have not been rightly informed, I will misinform you. The accounts of Naaman's death are overdrawn. He was killed, but his life has been preserved. One of his wounds was mortal, but the other three were curable, and by these the physicians have saved him.

SHUMAKIM: [*Balancing himself before* RAKHAZ *in pretended admiration.*]

O wonderful! Most admirable logic! One mortal, and three curable, therefore he must recover as it were, by three to one. Rakhaz, do you know that you are a marvelous man?

RAKHAZ:

Yes, I know it, but I make no boast of my knowledge.

SHUMAKIM:

Too modest, for in knowing this you know more than any other in Damascus!

[*Enter, from the right,* SABALLIDIN *in armour: from the left,* TSARPI *with her attendants, among whom is* RUAHMAH.]

HAZAEL:

Here is Saballidin, we'll question him;
He was enflamed by Naaman's wild words,
And rode with him to battle. Give us news,
Of your great captain! Is he safe and well?
When will he come? Or will he come at all?

[*All gather around him listening eagerly.*]

SABALLIDIN:

He comes but now, returning from the field
Where he hath gained a crown of deathless fame!
Three times he led the charge; three times he fell
Wounded, and the Assyrians beat us back.
Yet every wound was but a spur to urge
His valour onward. In the last attack

He rode before us as the crested wave
That leads the flood; and lo, our enemies
Were broken like a dam of river-reeds.
The flying King encircled by his guard
Was lodged like driftwood on a little hill.
Then Naaman, who led our foremost band
Of whirlwind riders, hammered through the hedge
Of spearmen, brandishing the golden yoke.
"Take back this gift," he cried; and shattered it
On Shalmaneser's helmet. So the fight
Dissolved in universal rout; the King,
His chariots and his horsemen fled away;
Our captain stood the master of the field,
And saviour of Damascus! Now he brings,
First to the King, report of this great triumph.

[*Shouts of joy and applause.*]

RUAHMAH: [*Coming close to* SABALLIDIN.]

But what of him who won it? Fares he well?
My mistress would receive some word of him.

SABALLIDIN:

Hath she not heard?

RUAHMAH:

But one brief message came:
A letter saying, "We have fought and conquered,"
No word of his own person. Fares he well?

SABALLIDIN:

Alas, most ill! For he is like a man
Consumed by some strange sickness: wasted, wan,—

His eyes are dimmed so that he scarce can see;
His ears are dulled; his fearless face is pale
As one who walks to meet a certain doom
Yet will not flinch. It is most pitiful,—
But you shall see.

RUAHMAH:

Yea, we shall see a man
Who dared to face the wrath of evil powers
Unknown, and hazard all to save his country.

[*Enter* BENHADAD *with courtiers.*]

BENHADAD:

Where is my faithful servant Naaman,
The captain of my host?

SABALLIDIN:

My lord, he comes.

[*Trumpet sounds. Enter company of soldiers in armour. Then four soldiers bearing captured standards of Asshur.* NAAMAN *follows, very pale, armour dinted and stained; he is blind, and guides himself by cords from the standards on each side, but walks firmly. The doors of the temple open slightly, and* REZON *appears at the top of the steps.* NAAMAN *lets the cords fall, and gropes his way for a few paces.*]

NAAMAN: [*Kneeling.*]

Where is my King?
Master, the bearer of thy sword returns.
The golden yoke thou gavest me I broke
On him who sent it. Asshur's Bull hath fled

Dehorned. The standards of his host are thine!
Damascus is all thine, at peace, and free!

BENHADAD: [*Holding out his arms.*]
Thou art a mighty man of valour! Come,
And let me fold thy courage to my heart.

REZON: [*Lifting his rod.*]
Forbear, O King! Stand back from him, all men!
By the great name of Rimmon I proclaim
This man a leper! See, upon his brow,
This little mark, the death-white seal of doom!
That tiny spot will spread, eating his flesh,
Gnawing his fingers bone from bone, until
The impious heart that dared defy the gods
Dissolves in the slow death which now begins.
Unclean! unclean! Henceforward he is dead:
No human hand shall touch him, and no home
Of men shall give him shelter. He shall walk
Only with corpses of the selfsame death
Down the long path to a forgotten tomb.
Avoid, depart, I do adjure you all,
Leave him to god,—the leper Naaman!

[*All shrink back horrified.* REZON *retires into the temple; the crowd melts away, wailing;* TSARPI *is among the first to go, followed by her attendants, except* RUAHMAH, *who crouches, with her face covered, not far from* NAAMAN.]

BENHADAD: [*Lingering and turning back.*]
Alas, my son! O Naaman, my son!
Why did I let thee go? I must obey.

Who can resist the gods? Yet none shall take
Thy glorious title, captain of my host!
I will provide for thee, and thou shalt dwell
With guards of honour in a house of mine
Always. Damascus never shall forget
What thou hast done! O miserable words
Of crowned impotence! O mockery of power
Given to kings who cannot even defend
Their dearest from the secret wrath of heaven!
O Naaman, my son, my son! [*Exit.*]

NAAMAN: [*Slowly passing his hand over his eyes, and looking up.*]

Am I alone
With thee, inexorable one, whose pride
Offended takes this horrible revenge?
I must submit my mortal flesh to thee,
Almighty, but I will not call thee god!
Yet thou hast found the way to wound my soul
Most deeply through the flesh; and I must find
The way to let my wounded soul escape!

[*Drawing his sword.*]

Come, my last friend, thou art more merciful
Than Rimmon. Why should I endure the doom
He sends me? Irretrievably cut off
From all dear intercourse of human love,
From all the tender touch of human hands,
From all brave comradeship with brother-men,
With eyes that see no faces through this dark,

With ears that hear all voices far away,
Why should I cling to misery, and grope
My long, long way from pain to pain, alone?

RUAHMAH: [*At his feet.*]

Nay, not alone, dear lord, for I am here;
And I will never leave thee, nor forsake thee!

NAAMAN:

What voice is that? The silence of my tomb
Is broken by a ray of music,—whose?

RUAHMAH: [*Rising.*]

The one who loves thee best in all the world.

NAAMAN:

Why that should be,—O dare I dream it true?
Tsarpi, my wife? Have I misjudged thy heart
As cold and proud? How nobly thou forgivest!
Thou com'st to hold me from the last disgrace,—
The coward's flight into the dark. Go back
Unstained, my sword! Life is endurable
While there is one alive on earth who loves us.

RUAHMAH:

My lord,—my lord,—O listen! You have erred,—
You do mistake me now,—this dream—

NAAMAN:

Ah, wake me not! For I can conquer death
Dreaming this dream. Let me at last believe,
Though gods are cruel, a woman can be kind.
Grant me but this! For see,—I ask so little,—

Only to know that thou art faithful,
That thou art near me, though I touch thee not,—
O this will hold me up, though it be given
From pity more than love.

RUAHMAH: [*Trembling, and speaking slowly.*]
Not so, my lord!
My pity is a stream; my pride of thee
Is like the sea that doth engulf the stream;
My love for thee is like the sovereign moon
That rules the sea. The tides that fill my soul
Flow unto thee and follow after thee;
And where thou goest I will go; and where
Thou diest I will die,—in the same hour.

[*She lays her hand on his arm. He draws back.*]

NAAMAN:
O touch me not! Thou shalt not share my doom.

RUAHMAH:
Entreat me not to go. I will obey
In all but this; but rob me not of this,—
The only boon that makes life worth the living,—
To walk beside thee day by day, and keep
Thy foot from stumbling; to prepare thy food
When thou art hungry, music for thy rest,
And cheerful words to comfort thy black hour;
And so to lead thee ever on, and on,
Through darkness, till we find the door of hope.

NAAMAN:
What word is that? The leper has no hope.

RUAHMAH:

Dear lord, the mark upon thy brow is yet
No broader than my little finger-nail.
Thy force is not abated, and thy step
Is firm. Wilt thou surrender to the enemy
Before thy strength is touched? Why, let me put
A drop of courage from my breast in thine!
There is a hope for thee. The captive maid
Of Israel who dwelt within thy house
Knew of a god very compassionate,
Long-suffering, slow to anger, one who heals
The sick, hath pity on the fatherless,
And saves the poor and him who has no helper.
His prophet dwells nigh to Samaria;
And I have heard that he hath brought the dead
To life again. We'll go to him. The King,
If I beseech him, will appoint a guard
Of thine own soldiers and Saballidin,
Thy friend, to convoy us upon our journey.
He'll give us royal letters to the King
Of Israel to make our welcome sure;
And we will take the open road, beneath
The open sky, to-morrow, and go on
Together till we find the door of hope.
Come, come with me!

[*She grasps his hand.*]

NAAMAN: [*Drawing back.*]

Thou must not touch me!

RUAHMAH: [*Unclasping her girdle and putting the end in his hand.*]

Take my girdle, then!

NAAMAN: [*Kissing the clasp of the girdle.*]

I do begin to think there is a God,
Since love on earth can work such miracles!

CURTAIN

ACT III

TIME: *A month later: dawn*

SCENE I

NAAMAN'S *tent, on high ground among the mountains near Samaria: the city below. In the distance, a wide and splendid landscape.* SABALLIDIN *and soldiers on guard below the tent. Enter* RUAHMAH *in hunter's dress, with a lute slung from her shoulder.*

RUAHMAH:

Peace and good health to you, Saballidin.
Good morrow to you all. How fares my lord?

SABALLIDIN:

The curtains of his tent are folded still:
They have not moved since we returned, last night,
And told him what befell us in the city.

RUAHMAH:

Told him! Why did you make report to him
And not to me? Am I not captain here,
Intrusted by the King's command with care
Of Naaman until he is restored?
'Tis mine to know the first of good or ill
In this adventure: mine to shield his heart
From every arrow of adversity.
What have you told him? Speak!

SABALLIDIN:

Lady, we feared
To bring our news to you. For when the King
Of Israel had read our monarch's letter,
He rent his clothes, and cried, "Am I a god,
To kill and make alive, that I should heal
A leper? Ye have come with false pretence,
Damascus seeks a quarrel with me. Go!"
But when we told our lord, he closed his tent,
And there remains enfolded in his grief.
I trust he sleeps; 'twere kind to let him sleep!
For now he doth forget his misery,
And all the burden of his hopeless woe
Is lifted from him by the gentle hand
Of slumber. Oh, to those bereft of hope
Sleep is the only blessing left,—the last
Asylum of the weary, the one sign
Of pity from impenetrable heaven.
Waking is strife; sleep is the truce of God!
Ah, lady, wake him not. The day will be
Full long for him to suffer, and for us
To turn our disappointed faces home
On the long road by which we must return.

RUAHMAH:

Return! Who gave you that command? Not I!
The King made me the leader of this quest,
And bound you all to follow me, because
He knew I never would return without

The thing for which he sent us. I'll go on
Day after day, unto the uttermost parts
Of earth, if need be, and beyond the gates
Of morning, till I find that which I seek,—
New life for Naaman. Are ye ashamed
To have a woman lead you? Then go back
And tell the King, "This huntress went too far
For us to follow: she pursues the trail
Of hope alone, refusing to forsake
The quarry: we grew weary of the chase;
And so we left her and retraced our steps,
Like faithless hounds, to sleep beside the fire."
Did Naaman forsake his soldiers thus
When you went forth to hunt the Assyrian Bull?
Your manly courage is less durable
Than woman's love, it seems. Go, if you will,—
Who bids me now farewell?

SOLDIERS:

Not I, not I!

SABALLIDIN:

Lady, lead on, we'll follow you forever!

RUAHMAH:

Why, now you speak like men! Brought you no word
Out of Samaria, except that cry
Of impotence and fear from Israel's King?

SABALLIDIN:

I do remember while he spoke with us

A rustic messenger came in, and cried
"Elisha saith, bring Naaman to me
At Dothan, he shall surely know there is
A God in Israel."

RUAHMAH:

What said the King?

SABALLIDIN:

He only shouted "Go!" more wildly yet,
And rent his clothes again, as if he were
Half-maddened by a coward's fear, and thought
Only of how he might be rid of us.
What comfort could there be for him, what hope
For us, in the rude prophet's misty word?

RUAHMAH:

It is the very word for which I prayed!
My trust was not in princes; for the crown,
The sceptre, and the purple robe are not
Significant of vital power. The man
Who saves his brother-men is he who lives
His life with Nature, takes deep hold on truth,
And trusts in God. A prophet's word is more
Than all the kings on earth can speak. How far
Is Dothan?

SOLDIER:

Lady, 'tis but three hours' ride
Along the valley southward.

RUAHMAH:

Near! so near?

I had not thought to end my task so soon!
Prepare yourselves with speed to take the road.
I will awake my lord.

[*Exeunt all but* SABALLIDIN *and* RUAHMAH. *She goes toward the tent.*]

SABALLIDIN:

Ruahmah, stay! [*She turns back.*]

I've been your servant in this doubtful quest,
Obedient, faithful, loyal to your will,—
What have I earned by this?

RUAHMAH:

The gratitude

Of him we both desire to serve: your friend,—
My master and my lord.

SABALLIDIN:

No more than this?

RUAHMAH:

Yes, if you will, take all the thanks my hands
Can hold, my lips can speak.

SABALLIDIN:

I would have more.

RUAHMAH:

My friend, there's nothing more to give to you.
My service to my lord is absolute.
There's not a drop of blood within my veins
But quickens at the very thought of him;
And not a dream of mine but he doth stand
Within its heart and make it bright. No man

To me is other than his friend or foe.
You are his friend, and I believe you true!

SABALLIDIN:

I have been true to him,—now, I am true
To you.

RUAHMAH:

Why, then, be doubly true to him.
O let us match our loyalties, and strive
Between us who shall win the higher crown!
Men boast them of a friendship stronger far
Than love of woman. Prove it! I'll not boast,
But I'll contend with you on equal terms
In this brave race: and if you win the prize
I'll hold you next to him: and if I win
He'll hold you next to me; and either way
We'll not be far apart. Do you accept
My challenge?

SABALLIDIN:

Yes! For you enforce my heart
By honour to resign its great desire,
And love itself to offer sacrifice
Of all disloyal dreams on its own altar.
Yet love remains; therefore I pray you, think
How surely you must lose in our contention.
For I am known to Naaman: but you
He blindly takes for Tsarpi. 'Tis to her
He gives his gratitude: the praise you win
Endears her name.

RUAHMAH:

Her name? Why, what is that?
A name is but an empty shell, a mask
That does not change the features of the face
Beneath it. Can a name rejoice, or weep,
Or hope? Can it be moved by tenderness
To daily services of love, or feel the warmth
Of dear companionship? How many things
We call by names that have no meaning! Kings
That cannot rule; and gods that are not good;
And wives that do not love! It matters not
What syllables he utters when he calls,
'Tis I who come,—'tis I who minister
Unto my lord, and mine the living heart
That feels the comfort of his confidence,
The thrill of gladness when he speaks to me,—
I do not hear the name!

SABALLIDIN:

And yet, be sure
There's danger in this error,—and no gain!

RUAHMAH:

I seek no gain: I only tread the path
Marked for me daily by the hand of love.
And if his blindness spared my lord one pang
Of sorrow in his black, forsaken hour,—
And if this error makes his burdened heart
More quiet, and his shadowed way less dark,
Whom do I rob? Not her who chose to stay

At ease in Rimmon's House! Surely not him!
Only myself! And that enriches me.
Why trouble we the master? Let it go,—
To-morrow he must know the truth,—and then
He shall dispose of me e'en as he will!

SABALLIDIN:

To-morrow?

RUAHMAH:

Yes, for I will tarry here,
While you conduct him to Elisha's house
To find the promised healing. I forebode
A sudden danger from the craven King
Of Israel, or else a secret ambush
From those who hate us in Damascus. Go,
But leave me twenty men: this mountain-pass
Protects the road behind you. Make my lord
Obey the prophet's word, whatever he commands,
And come again in peace. Farewell!

[*Exit* SABALLIDIN. RUAHMAH *goes toward the tent, then pauses and turns back. She takes her lute and sings.*]

SONG

Above the edge of dark appear the lances of the sun;
Along the mountain-ridges clear his rosy heralds run;
The vapours down the valley go
Like broken armies, dark and low.
Look up, my heart, from every hill

In folds of rose and daffodil
The sunrise banners flow.

O fly away on silent wing, ye boding owls of night!
O welcome little birds that sing the coming-in of light!
For new, and new, and ever-new,
The golden bud within the blue;
And every morning seems to say:
"There's something happy on the way,
"And God sends love to you!"

NAAMAN: [*Appearing at the entrance of his tent.*]
O let me ever wake to music! For the soul
Returns most gently then, and finds its way
By the soft, winding clue of melody,
Out of the dusky labyrinth of sleep,
Into the light. My body feels the sun
Though I behold naught that his rays reveal.
Come, thou who art my daydawn and my sight,
Sweet eyes, come close, and make the sunrise mine!

RUAHMAH: [*Coming near.*]
A fairer day, dear lord, was never born
In Paradise! The sapphire cup of heaven
Is filled with golden wine: the earth, adorned
With jewel-drops of dew, unveils her face
A joyful bride, in welcome to her king.
And look! He leaps upon the Eastern hills
All ruddy fire, and claims her with a kiss.

Yonder the snowy peaks of Hermon float
Unmoving as a wind-dropt cloud. The gulf
Of Jordan, filled with violet haze, conceals
The river's winding trail with wreaths of mist.
Below us, marble-crowned Samaria thrones
Upon her emerald hill amid the Vale
Of Barley, while the plains to northward change
Their colour like the shimmering necks of doves.
The lark springs up, with morning on her wings,
To climb her singing stairway in the blue,
And all the fields are sprinkled with her joy!

NAAMAN:

Thy voice is magical: thy words are visions!
I must content myself with them, for now
My only hope is lost: Samaria's King
Rejects our monarch's message,—hast thou heard?
"Am I a god that I should cure a leper?"
He sends me home unhealed, with angry words,
Back to Damascus and the lingering death.

RUAHMAH:

What matter where he sends? No god is he
To slay or make alive. Elisha bids
You come to him at Dothan, there to learn
There is a God in Israel.

NAAMAN:

I fear
That I am grown mistrustful of all gods;
Their secret counsels are implacable.

RUAHMAH:

Fear not! There's One who rules in righteousness
High over all.

NAAMAN:

What knowest thou of Him?

RUAHMAH:

Oh, I have heard,—the maid of Israel,—
Rememberest thou? She often said her God
Was merciful and kind, and slow to wrath,
And plenteous in forgiveness, pitying us
Like as a father pitieth his children.

NAAMAN:

If there were such a God, I'd worship Him
Forever!

RUAHMAH:

Then make haste to hear the word
His prophet promises to speak to thee!
Obey it, my dear lord, and thou shalt find
Healing and peace. The light shall fill thine eyes.
Thou wilt not need my leading any more,—
Nor me,—for thou wilt see me, all unveiled,—
I tremble at the thought.

NAAMAN:

Why, what is this?
Why shouldst thou tremble? Art thou not mine
own?

RUAHMAH: [*Turning to him and speaking in broken words.*]

I am,—thy handmaid,—all and only thine,—

The very pulses of my heart are thine!
Feel how they throb to comfort thee to-day—
To-day! Because it is thy time of trouble.

[*She takes his hand and puts it to her forehead and her lips, but before she can lay it upon her heart, he draws away from her.*]

NAAMAN:

Thou art too dear to injure with a kiss,—
How should I take a gift may bankrupt thee,
Or drain the fragrant chalice of thy love
With lips that may be fatal? Tempt me not
To sweet dishonour; strengthen me to wait
Until thy prophecy is all fulfilled,
And I can claim thee with a joyful heart.

RUAHMAH: [*Turning away.*]

Thou wilt not need me then,—and I shall be
No more than the faint echo of a song
Heard half asleep. We shall go back to where
We stood before this journey.

NAAMAN:

Never again!
For thou art changed by some deep miracle.
The flower of womanhood hath bloomed in thee,—
Art thou not changed?

RUAHMAH:

Yea, I am changed,—and changed
Again,—bewildered,—till there's nothing clear
To me but this: I am the instrument

In an Almighty hand to rescue thee
From death. This will I do,—and afterward—
[*A trumpet is blown without.*]
Hearken, the trumpet sounds, the chariot waits.
Away, dear lord, follow the road to light!

SCENE II *

The house of Elisha, upon a terraced hillside. A low stone cottage with vine-trellises and flowers; a flight of steps, at the foot of which is NAAMAN'S *chariot. He is standing in it;* SABALLIDIN *beside it. Two soldiers come down the steps.*

FIRST SOLDIER:
We have delivered my lord's greeting and his message.

SECOND SOLDIER:
Yes, and near lost our noses in the doing of it! For the servant slammed the door in our faces. A most unmannerly reception!

FIRST SOLDIER:
But I take that as a good omen. It is a mark of holy men to keep ill-conditioned servants. Look, the door opens, the prophet is coming.

SECOND SOLDIER:
No, by my head, it is that notable mark of his mas-

* Note that this scene is not intended to be put upon the stage, the effect of the action upon the drama being given at the beginning of Act IV.

ter's holiness, that same lantern-jawed lout of a servant.

[GEHAZI *loiters down the steps and comes to* NAAMAN *with a slight obeisance.*]

GEHAZI:

My master, the prophet of Israel, sends word to Naaman the Syrian,—are you he?—"Go wash in Jordan seven times and be healed."

[GEHAZI *turns and goes slowly up the steps.*]

NAAMAN:

What insolence is this? Am I a man
To be put off with surly messengers?
Has not Damascus rivers more renowned
Than this rude muddy Jordan? Crystal streams,
Abana! Pharpar! flowing smoothly through
A paradise of roses? Might I not
Have bathed in them and been restored at ease?
Come up, Saballidin, and guide me home!

SABALLIDIN:

Bethink thee, master, shall we lose our quest
Because a servant is uncouth? The road
That seeks the mountain leads us through the vale.
The prophet's word is friendly after all;
For had it been some mighty task he set,
Thou wouldst perform it. How much rather then
This easy one? Hast thou not promised her
Who waits for thy return? Wilt thou go back
To her unhealed?

NAAMAN:

No! not for all my pride!
I'll make myself most humble for her sake,
And stoop to anything that gives me hope
Of having her. Make haste, Saballidin,
Bring me to Jordan. I will cast myself
Into that river's turbulent embrace
A hundred times, until I save my life
Or lose it!

[*Exeunt. The light fades: musical interlude. The light increases again with ruddy sunset shining on the door of* ELISHA'S *house. The prophet appears and looks off, shading his eyes with his hand as he descends the steps. Trumpet blows,—*NAAMAN'S *call;—sound of horses galloping and men shouting.* NAAMAN *enters joyously, followed by* SABALLIDIN *and soldiers, with gifts.*]

NAAMAN:

Behold a man delivered from the grave
By thee! I rose from Jordan's waves restored
To youth and vigour, as the eagle mounts
Upon the sunbeam and renews his strength!
O mighty prophet deign to take from me
These gifts too poor to speak my gratitude;
Silver and gold and jewels, damask robes,—

ELISHA: [*Interrupting.*]

As thy soul liveth I will not receive

A gift from thee, my son! Give all to Him
Whose mercy hath redeemed thee from thy plague.

NAAMAN:

He is the only God! I worship Him!
Grant me a portion of the blessed soil
Of this most favoured land where I have found
His mercy; in Damascus will I build
An altar to His name, and praise Him there
Morning and night. There is no other God
In all the world.

ELISHA:

Thou needst not
This load of earth to build a shrine for Him;
Yet take it if thou wilt. But be assured
God's altar is in every loyal heart,
And every flame of love that kindles there
Ascends to Him and brightens with His praise.
There is no other God! But evil Powers
Make war against Him in the darkened world;
And many temples have been built to them.

NAAMAN:

I know them well! Yet when my master goes
To worship in the House of Rimmon, I
Must enter with him; for he trusts me, leans
Upon my hand; and when he bows himself
I cannot help but make obeisance too,—
But not to Rimmon! To my country's King

I'll bow in love and honour. Will the Lord
Pardon thy servant in this thing?

ELISHA:

My son,
Peace has been granted thee. 'Tis thine to find
The only way to keep it. Go in peace.

NAAMAN:

Thou hast not answered me,—may I bow down?

ELISHA:

The answer must be thine. The heart that knows
The perfect peace of gratitude and love,
Walks in the light and needs no other rule.
When next thou comest into Rimmon's House,
Thy heart will tell thee how to go in peace.

CURTAIN

ACT IV

SCENE I

The interior of NAAMAN'S *tent, at night.* RUAHMAH *alone, sleeping on the ground. A vision appears to her through the curtains of the tent:* ELISHA *standing on the hillside at Dothan:* NAAMAN, *restored to sight, comes in and kneels before him.* ELISHA *blesses him, and he goes out rejoicing. The vision of the prophet turns to* RUAHMAH *and lifts his hand in warning.*

ELISHA:

Daughter of Israel, what dost thou here?
Thy prayer is granted. Naaman is healed:
Mar not true service with a selfish thought.
Nothing remains for thee to do, except
Give thanks, and go whither the Lord commands.
Obey,—obey! Ere Naaman returns
Thou must depart to thine own house in Shechem.

[*The vision vanishes.*]

RUAHMAH: [*Waking and rising slowly.*]

A dream, a dream, a messenger of God!
O dear and dreadful vision, art thou true?
Then am I glad with all my broken heart.
Nothing remains,—nothing remains but this,—
Give thanks, obey, depart,—and so I do.

Farewell, my master's sword! Farewell to you,
My amulet! I lay you on the hilt
His hand shall clasp again: bid him farewell
For me, since I must look upon his face
No more for ever!—Hark, what sound was that?
[*Enter soldier hurriedly.*]

SOLDIER:
Mistress, an armèd troop, footmen and horse,
Mounting the hill!

RUAHMAH:
My lord returns in triumph.

SOLDIER:
Not so, for these are enemies; they march
In haste and silence, answering not our cries.

RUAHMAH:
Our enemies? Then hold your ground,—on guard!
Fight! fight! Defend the pass, and drive them down.
[*Exit soldier.* RUAHMAH *draws* NAAMAN'S *sword from the scabbard and hurries out of the tent. Confused noise of fighting outside. Three or four soldiers are driven in by a troop of men in disguise.* RUAHMAH *follows: she is beaten to her knees, and her sword is broken.*]

REZON: [*Throwing aside the cloth which covers his face.*]
Hold her! So, tiger-maid, we've found your lair
And trapped you. Where is Naaman,
Your master?

RUAHMAH: [*Rising, her arms held by two of* REZON'S *followers.*]

He is far beyond your reach.

REZON:

Brave captain! He has saved himself, the leper,
And left you here?

RUAHMAH:

The leper is no more.

REZON:

What mean you?

RUAHMAH:

He has gone to meet his God.

REZON:

Dead? Dead? Behold how Rimmon's wrath is swift!
Damascus shall be mine; I'll terrify
The King with this, and make my terms. But no!
False maid, you sweet-faced harlot, you have lied
To save him,—speak.

RUAHMAH:

I am not what you say,
Nor have I lied, nor will I ever speak
A word to you, vile servant of a traitor-god.

REZON:

Break off this little flute of blasphemy,
This ivory neck,—twist it, I say!
Give her a swift despatch after her leper!
But stay,—if he still lives he'll follow her,
And so we may ensnare him. Harm her not!

Bind her! Away with her to Rimmon's House!
Is all this carrion dead? There's one that moves,—
A spear,—fasten him down! All quiet now?
Then back to our Damascus! Rimmon's face
Shall be made bright with sacrifice.

[*Exeunt, forcing* RUAHMAH *with them. Musical interlude. A wounded soldier crawls from a dark corner of the tent and finds the chain with* NAAMAN'S *seal, which has fallen to the ground in the struggle.*]

WOUNDED SOLDIER:

The signet of my lord, her amulet!
Lost, lost! Ah, noble lady,—let me die
With this upon my breast.

[*The tent is dark. Enter* NAAMAN *and his company in haste, with torches.*]

NAAMAN:

What bloody work
Is here? God, let me live to punish him
Who wrought this horror! Treacherously slain
At night, by unknown hands, my brave companions:
Tsarpi, my best beloved, light of my soul,
Put out in darkness! O my broken lamp
Of life, where art thou? Nay, I cannot find her.

WOUNDED SOLDIER: [*Raising himself on his arm.*]

Master!

NAAMAN: [*Kneels beside him.*]

One living? Quick, a torch this way!

Lift up his head,—so,—carefully!
Courage, my friend, your captain is beside you.
Call back your soul and make report to him.

WOUNDED SOLDIER:
Hail, captain! O my captain,—here!

NAAMAN:
Be patient,—rest in peace,—the fight is done.
Nothing remains but render your account.

WOUNDED SOLDIER:
They fell upon us suddenly,—we fought
Our fiercest,—every man,—our lady fought
Fiercer than all. They beat us down,—she's gone.
Rezon has carried her away a captive. See,—
Her amulet,—I die for you, my captain.

NAAMAN: [*He gently lays the dead soldier on the ground, and rises.*]
Farewell. This last report was brave; but strange
Beyond my thought! How came the High Priest here?
And what is this? my chain, my seal! But this
Has never been in Tsarpi's hand. I gave
This signet to a captive maid one night,—
A maid of Israel. How long ago?
Ruahmah was her name,—almost forgotten!
So long ago,—how comes this token here?
What is this mystery, Saballidin?

SABALLIDIN:
Ruahmah is her name who brought you hither.

NAAMAN:

Where then is Tsarpi?

SABALLIDIN:

In Damascus.

She left you when the curse of Rimmon fell,—
Took refuge in his House,—and there she waits
Her lord's return,—Rezon's return.

NAAMAN:

'Tis false!

SABALLIDIN:

The falsehood is in her. She hath been friend
With Rezon in his priestly plot to win
Assyria's favour,—friend to his design
To sell his country to enrich his temple,—
And friend to him in more,—I will not name it.

NAAMAN:

Nor will I credit it. Impossible!

SABALLIDIN:

Did she not plead with you against the war,
Counsel surrender, seek to break your will?

NAAMAN:

She did not love my work, a soldier's task.
She never seemed to be at one with me
Until I was a leper.

SABALLIDIN:

From whose hand

Did you receive the sacred cup?

NAAMAN:

From hers.

SABALLIDIN:

And from that hour the curse began to work.

NAAMAN:

But did she not have pity when she saw
Me smitten? Did she not beseech the King
For letters and a guard to make this journey?
Has she not been the fountain of my hope,
My comforter and my most faithful guide
In this adventure of the dark? All this
Is proof of perfect love that would have shared
A leper's doom rather than give me up.
Can I doubt her who dared to love like this?

SABALLIDIN:

O master, doubt her not,—but know her name;
Ruahmah! It was she alone who wrought
This wondrous work of love. She won the King
To furnish forth this company. She led
Our march, kept us in heart, fought off despair,
Watched over you as if you were her child,
Prepared your food, your cup, with her own hands,
Sang you asleep at night, awake at dawn,—

NAAMAN: [*Interrupting.*]

Enough! I do remember every hour
Of that sweet comradeship! And now her voice
Wakens the echoes in my lonely breast.
Shall I not see her, thank her, speak her name?
Ruahmah! Let me live till I have looked
Into her eyes and called her my Ruahmah!

[*To his soldiers.*]
Away! away! I burn to take the road
That leads me back to Rimmon's House,—
But not to bow,—by God, never to bow!

SCENE II

TIME: *Three days later*

Inner court of the House of Rimmon; a temple with huge pillars at each side. In the right foreground the seat of the King; at the left, of equal height, the seat of the High Priest. In the background a broad flight of steps, rising to a curtain of cloudy gray, embroidered with two gigantic hands holding thunderbolts. The temple is in half darkness at first. Enter KHAMMA *and* NUBTA, *robed as Kharimati, or religious dancers, in gowns of black gauze with yellow embroideries and mantles.*

KHAMMA:
All is ready for the rites of worship; our lady will play a great part in them. She has put on her Tyrian robes, and all her ornaments.

NUBTA:
That is a sure sign of a religious purpose. She is most devout, our lady Tsarpi!

KHAMMA:
A favourite of Rimmon, too! The High Priest has assured her of it. He is a great man,—next to the King, now that Naaman is gone.

NUBTA:

But if Naaman should come back, healed of the leprosy?

KHAMMA:

How can he come back? The Hebrew slave that went away with him, when they caught her, said that he was dead. The High Priest has shut her up in the prison of the temple, accusing her of her master's death.

NUBTA:

Yet I think he does not believe it, for I heard him telling our mistress what to do if Naaman should return.

KHAMMA:

What, then?

NUBTA:

She will claim him as her husband. Was she not wedded to him before the god? That is a sacred bond. Only the High Priest can loose it. She will keep her hold on Naaman for the sake of the House of Rimmon. A wife knows her husband's secrets, she can tell——

[*Enter* SHUMAKIM, *with his flagon, walking unsteadily.*]

KHAMMA:

Hush! here comes the fool Shumakim. He is never sober.

SHUMAKIM: [*Laughing.*]

Are there two of you? I see two, but that is no proof. I think there is only one, but beautiful enough for two. What were you talking to yourself about, fairest one!

KHAMMA:

About the lady Tsarpi, fool, and what she would do if her husband returned.

SHUMAKIM:

Fie! fie! That is no talk for an innocent fool to hear. Has she a husband?

NUBTA:

You know very well that she is the wife of Lord Naaman.

SHUMAKIM:

I remember that she used to wear his name and his jewels. But I thought he had exchanged her,—for a leprosy.

KHAMMA:

You must have heard that he went away to Samaria to look for healing. Some say that he died on the journey; but others say he has been cured, and is on his way home to his wife.

SHUMAKIM:

It may be, for this is a mad world, and men never know when they are well off,—except us fools. But he must come soon if he would find his wife as he parted from her,—or the city where he left it. The Assyrians have returned with a greater army, and this time they will make an end of us. There is no Naaman now, and the Bull will devour Damascus like a bunch of leeks, flowers and all,—flowers and all, my double-budded fair one! Are you not afraid?

NUBTA:

We belong to the House of Rimmon. He will protect us.

SHUMAKIM:

What? The mighty one who hides behind the curtain there, and tells his secrets to Rezon? No doubt he will take care of you, and of himself. Whatever game is played, the gods never lose. But for the protection of the common people and the rest of us fools, I would rather have Naaman at the head of an army than all the sacred images between here and Babylon.

KHAMMA:

You are a wicked old man. You mock the god. He will punish you.

SHUMAKIM: [*Bitterly.*]

How can he punish me? Has he not already made me a fool? Hark, here comes my brother the High Priest, and my brother the King. Rimmon made us all; but nobody knows who made Rimmon, except the High Priest; and he will never tell.

Gongs and cymbals sound. Enter REZON *with priests, and*

the King with courtiers. They take their seats. A throng of Khali and Kharimati come in, TSARPI *presiding; a sacred dance is performed with torches, burning incense, and chanting, in which* TSARPI *leads.*]

CHANT

Hail, mighty Rimmon, ruler of the whirl-storm,
Hail, shaker of mountains, breaker-down of forests,
Hail, thou who roarest terribly in the darkness,
Hail, thou whose arrows flame across the heavens!
Hail, great destroyer, lord of flood and tempest,
In thine anger almighty, in thy wrath eternal,
Thou who delightest in ruin, maker of desolations,
Immeru, Addu, Berku, Rimmon!
See we tremble before thee, low we bow at thine altar,
Have mercy upon us, be favourable unto us,
Save us from our enemy, accept our sacrifice,
Barku, Immeru, Addu, Rimmon!
[*Silence follows, all bowing down.*]

REZON:

O King, last night the counsel from above
Was given in answer to our divination.
Ambassadors must go forthwith to crave
Assyria's pardon, and a second offer
Of the same terms of peace we did reject
Not long ago.

BENHADAD:

Dishonour! Yet I see

No other way! Assyria will refuse,
Or make still harder terms. Disaster, shame
For this gray head, and ruin for Damascus!

REZON:

Yet may we trust Rimmon will favour us,
If we adhere devoutly to his worship.
He will incline his brother-god, the Bull,
To spare us, if we supplicate him now
With costly gifts. Therefore I have prepared
A sacrifice: Rimmon shall be well pleased
With the red blood that bathes his knees to-night!

BENHADAD:

My mind is dark with doubt,—I do forebode
Some horror! Let me go,—I am an old man,—
If Naaman my captain were alive!
But he is dead,—the glory is departed!

[*He rises, trembling, to leave the throne. Trumpet sounds,*—NAAMAN'S *call;—enter* NAAMAN, *followed by soldiers; he kneels at the foot of the throne.*]

BENHADAD: [*Half-whispering.*]

Art thou a ghost escaped from Allatu?
How didst thou pass the seven doors of death?
O noble ghost I am afraid of thee,
And yet I love thee,—let me hear thy voice!

NAAMAN:

No ghost, my King, but one who lives to serve
Thee and Damascus with his heart and sword

As in the former days. The only God
Has healed my leprosy: my life is clean
To offer to my country and my King.

BENHADAD: [*Starting toward him.*]
O welcome to thy King! Thrice welcome!

REZON: [*Leaving his seat and coming toward* NAAMAN.]
Stay!
The leper must appear before the priest,
The only one who can pronounce him clean.
[NAAMAN *turns; they stand looking each other in the face.*]
Yea,—thou art cleansed: Rimmon hath pardoned thee,—
In answer to the daily prayers of her
Whom he restores to thine embrace,—thy wife.
[TSARPI *comes slowly toward* NAAMAN.]

NAAMAN:
From him who rules this House will I receive
Nothing! I seek no pardon from his priest,
No wife of mine among his votaries!

TSARPI: [*Holding out her hands.*]
Am I not yours? Will you renounce our vows?

NAAMAN:
The vows were empty,—never made you mine
In aught but name. A wife is one who shares
Her husband's thought, incorporates his heart
With hers by love, and crowns him with her trust.
She is God's remedy for loneliness,

And God's reward for all the toil of life.
This you have never been to me,—and so
I give you back again to Rimmon's House
Where you belong. Claim what you will of mine,—
Not me! I do renounce you,—or release you,—
According to the law. If you demand
A further cause than what I have declared,
I will unfold it fully to the King.

REZON: [*Interposing hurriedly.*]
No need of that! This duteous lady yields
To your caprice as she has ever done:
She stands a monument of loyalty
And woman's meekness.

NAAMAN:
Let her stand for that!
Adorn your temple with her piety!
But you in turn restore to me the treasure
You stole at midnight from my tent.

REZON:
What treasure! I have stolen none from you.

NAAMAN:
The very jewel of my soul,—Ruahmah!
My King, the captive maid of Israel,
To whom thou didst commit my broken life
With letters to Samaria,—my light,
My guide, my saviour in this pilgrimage,—
Dost thou remember?

BENHADAD:

I recall the maid,—
But dimly,—for my mind is old and weary,
She was a fearless maid, I trusted her
And gave thee to her charge. Where is she now?

NAAMAN:

This robber fell upon my camp by night,—
While I was with Elisha at the Jordan,—
Slaughtered my soldiers, carried off the maid,
And holds her somewhere in imprisonment.
O give this jewel back to me, my King,
And I will serve thee with a grateful heart
For ever. I will fight for thee, and lead
Thine armies on to glorious victory
Over all foes! Thou shalt no longer fear
The host of Asshur, for thy throne shall stand
Encompassed with a wall of dauntless hearts,
And founded on a mighty people's love,
And guarded by the God of righteousness.

BENHADAD:

I feel the flame of courage at thy breath
Leap up among the ashes of despair.
Thou hast returned to save us! Thou shalt have
The maid; and thou shalt lead my host again!
Priest, I command you give her back to him.

REZON:

O master, I obey thy word as thou
Hast ever been obedient to the voice

Of Rimmon. Let thy fiery captain wait
Until the sacrifice has been performed,
And he shall have the jewel that he claims.
Must we not first placate the city's god
With due allegiance, keep the ancient faith,
And pay our homage to the Lord of Wrath?

BENHADAD: [*Sinking back upon his throne in fear.*]
I am the faithful son of Rimmon's House,—
And lo, these many years I worship him!
My thoughts are troubled,—I am very old,
But still a King! O Naaman, be patient!
Priest, let the sacrifice be offered.

[*The High Priest lifts his rod. Gongs and cymbals sound. The curtain is rolled back, disclosing the image of Rimmon; a gigantic and hideous idol, with a cruel human face, four horns, the mane of a lion, and huge paws stretched in front of him enclosing a low altar of black stone.* RUAHMAH *stands on the altar, chained, her arms are bare and folded on her breast. The people prostrate themselves in silence, with signs of astonishment and horror.*]

REZON:
Behold the sacrifice! Bow down, bow down!

NAAMAN: [*Stabbing him.*]
Bow thou, black priest! Down,—down to hell!
Ruahmah! do not die! I come to thee.

[NAAMAN *rushes toward her, attacked by the priests, crying "Sacrilege! Kill him!" But the sol-*

diers stand on the steps and beat them back. He springs upon the altar and clasps her by the hand. Tumult and confusion. The King rises and speaks with a loud voice, silence follows.]

BENHADAD:

Peace, peace! The King commands all weapons down!
O Naaman, what wouldst thou do? Beware
Lest thou provoke the anger of a god.

NAAMAN:

There is no God but one, the Merciful,
Who gave this perfect woman to my soul
That I might learn through her to worship Him,
And know the meaning of immortal Love.

BENHADAD: [*Agitated.*]

Yet she is consecrated, bound, and doomed
To sacrificial death; but thou art sworn
To live and lead my host,—Hast thou not sworn?

NAAMAN:

Only if thou wilt keep thy word to me!
Break with this idol of iniquity
Whose shadow makes a darkness in the land;
Give her to me who gave me back to thee;
And I will lead thine army to renown
And plant thy banners on the hill of triumph.
But if she dies, I die with her, defying Rimmon.

[*Cries of "Spare them! Release her! Give us back our Captain!" and "Sacrilege! Let them die!" Then silence, all turning toward the King.*]

BENHADAD:

Is this the choice? Must we destroy the bond
Of ancient faith, or slay the city's living hope!
I am an old, old man,—and yet the King!
Must I decide?—O let me ponder it!

[*His head sinks upon his breast. All stand eagerly looking at him.*]

NAAMAN:

Ruahmah, my Ruahmah! I have come
To thee at last! And art thou satisfied?

RUAHMAH: [*Looking into his face.*]

Belovéd, my belovéd, I am glad
Of all, and glad for ever, come what may.
Nothing can harm me,—since my lord is come!

APPENDIX

CARMINA FESTIVA

THE LITTLE-NECK CLAM

A modern verse-sequence, showing how a native American subject, strictly realistic, may be treated in various manners adapted to the requirements of different magazines, thus combining Art-for-Art's-Sake with Writing-for-the-Market. Read at the First Dinner of the American Periodical Publishers' Association, in Washington, April, 1904.

I

THE ANTI-TRUST CLAM

For *McClure's Magazine*

THE clam that once, on Jersey's banks,
Was like the man who dug it, free,
Now slave-like thro' the market clanks
In chains of corporate tyranny.

The Standard Fish-Trust of New York
Holds every clam-bank in control;
And like base Beef and menial Pork,
The free-born Clam has lost its soul.

No more the bivalve treads the sands
In freedom's rapture, free from guilt:
It follows now the harsh commands
Of Morgiman and Rockabilt.

Rise, freemen, rise! Your wrath is just!
Call on the Sherman Act to dam
The floods of this devouring Trust,
And liberate the fettered Clam.

CARMINA FESTIVA

II

The Whitmaniac Clam

For the *Bookman*

Not Dante when he wandered by the river Arno,
Not Burns who plowed the banks and braes of bonnie
 Ayr,
Not even Shakspere on the shores of Avon,—ah, no!
Not one of those great bards did taste true Poet's Fare.

But Whitman, loafing in Long Island and New Jersey,
Found there the sustenance of mighty ode and psalm,
And while his rude emotions swam around in verse, he
Fed chiefly on the wild, impassioned, sea-born clam.

Thus in his work we feel the waves' bewildering motion,
And winds from mighty mud-flats, weird and wild:
His clam-filled bosom answered to the voice of ocean,
And rose and fell responsively with every tide.

THE LITTLE-NECK CLAM

III

Il Mercatore Italiano Della Clamma

For the *Century Magazine*

"Clam O! Fres' Clam!" How strange it sounds and
sweet,
The Dago's cry along the New York street!
"Dago" we call him, like the thoughtless crowd;
And yet this humble man may well be proud
To hail from Petrarch's land, Boccaccio's home,—
Firenze, Gubbio, Venezia, Rome,—
From fair Italia, whose enchanted soil
Transforms the lowly cotton-seed to olive-oil.

To me his chant, with alien accent sung,
Brings back an echo of great Virgil's tongue:
It seems to cry against the city's woe,
In liquid Latin syllables,—*Clamo!*
As thro' the crowded street his cart he jams
And cries aloud, ah, think of more than clams!
Receive his secret plaint with pity warm,
And grant Italia's plea for Tenement-House Reform!

CARMINA FESTIVA

IV

The Social Clam

For the *Smart Set*

Fair Phyllis is another's bride:
Therefore I like to sit beside
Her at a very smart set dinner,
And whisper love, and try to win her.

The little-necks,—in number six,—
That from their pearly shells she picks
And swallows whole,—ah, is it selfish
To wish my heart among those shell-fish?

"But Phyllis is another's wife;
And if she should absorb thy life
'T would leave thy bosom vacant."—Well,
I'd keep at least the empty shell!

V

The Recreant Clam

For the *Outlook*

Low dost thou lie amid the languid ooze,
Because thy slothful spirit doth refuse
The bliss of battle and the strain of strife.
Rise, craven clam, and lead the strenuous life!

A FAIRY TALE

For the Mark Twain Dinner, December 5, 1905

SOME three-score years and ten ago
A prince was born at Florida, Mo.;
And though he came *incognito,*
With just the usual yells of woe,
The watchful fairies seemed to know
Precisely what the row meant;
For when he was but five days old,
(December fifth as I've been told,)
They pattered through the midnight cold,
And came around his crib, to hold
A Council of Endowment."

"I give him Wit," the eldest said,
And stooped above the little bed,
To touch his forehead round and red.
"Within this bald, unfurnished head,
"Where wild luxuriant locks shall spread
"And wave in years hereafter,
"I kindle now the lively spark,
"That still shall flash by day and dark,
"And everywhere he goes shall mark
"His way with light and laughter."

The fairies laughed to think of it
That such a rosy, wrinkled bit
Of flesh should be endowed with Wit!
But something serious seemed to hit
The mind of one, as if a fit
        Of fear had come upon her.
"I give him Truth," she quickly cried,
"That laughter may not lead aside
"To paths where scorn and falsehood hide,—
        "I give him Truth and Honour!"

"I give him Love," exclaimed the third;
And as she breathed the mystic word,
I know not if the baby heard,
But softly in his dream he stirred,
And twittered like a little bird,
        And stretched his hands above him.
The fairy's gift was sealed and signed
With kisses twain the deed to bind:
"A heart of love to human-kind,
        "And human-kind to love him!"

A FAIRY TALE

"Now stay your giving!" cried the Queen.
"These gifts are passing rich I ween;
"And if reporters should be mean
"Enough to spy upon this scene,
"'Twould make all other babies green
"With envy at the rumour.
"Yet since I love this child, forsooth,
"I'll mix your gifts, Wit, Love and Truth,
"With spirits of Immortal Youth,
"And call the mixture Humour!"

The fairies vanished with their glittering train;
But here's the Prince with all their gifts,—*Mark Twain.*

THE BALLAD OF THE SOLEMN ASS

Recited at the Century Club, New York: Twelfth Night. 1906

Come all ye good Centurions and wise men of the times,
You've made a Poet Laureate, now you must hear his rhymes.
Extend your ears and I'll respond by shortening up my tale:—
Man cannot live by verse alone, he must have cakes and ale.

So while you wait for better things and muse on schnapps and salad,
I'll try my Pegasus his wings and sing a little ballad:
A legend of your ancestors, the Wise Men of the East,
Who brought among their baggage train a quaint and curious beast.

Their horses were both swift and strong, and we should think it lucky
If we could buy, by telephone, such horses from Kentucky;
Their dromedaries paced along, magnificent and large,
Their camels were as stately as if painted by La Farge.

But this amazing little ass was never satisfied,
He made more trouble every day than all the rest beside:

THE BALLAD OF THE SOLEMN ASS

His ears were long, his legs were short, his eyes were
bleared and dim,
But nothing in the wide, wide world was good enough
for him.

He did not like the way they went, but lifted up his
voice
And said that any other way would be a better choice.
He braced his feet and stood his ground, and made the
wise men wait,
While with his heels at all around he did recalcitrate.

It mattered not how fair the land through which the
road might run,
He found new causes for complaint with every Morning
Sun:
And when the shades of twilight fell and all the world
grew nappy,
They tied him to his Evening Post, but still he was not
happy.

He thought his load was far too large, he thought his
food was bad,
He thought the Star a poor affair, he thought the Wise
Men mad:
He did not like to hear them laugh,—'twas childish to
be jolly;
And if perchance they sang a hymn,—'twas sentimental
folly!

So day by day this little beast performed his level best
To make their life, in work and play, a burden to the rest:
And when they laid them down at night, he would not let them sleep,
But criticized the Universe with hee-haws loud and deep.

One evening, as the Wise Men sat before their fire-lit tent,
And ate and drank and talked and sang, in grateful merriment,
The solemn donkey butted in, in his most solemn way,
And broke the happy meeting up with a portentous bray.

"Now by my head," Balthazar said (his real name was Choate),
"We've had about enough of this! I'll put it to the vote.
"I move the donkey be dismissed; let's turn him out to grass,
"And travel on our cheerful way, without the solemn ass."

The vote was aye! and with a whack the Wise Men drove him out;
But still he wanders up and down, and all the world about;
You'll know him by his long, sad face and supercilious ways,
And likewise by his morning kicks and by his evening brays.

THE BALLAD OF THE SOLEMN ASS

But while we sit at Eagle Roost and make our Twelfth
 Night cheer,
Full well we know the solemn ass will not disturb us here:
For pleasure rules the roost to-night, by order of the
 King,
And every one must play his part, and laugh, and like-
 wise sing.

The road of life is long, we know, and often hard to find,
And yet there's many a pleasant turn for men of cheerful mind:
We've done our day's work honestly, we've earned the
 right to rest,
We'll take a cup of friendship now and spice it with a
 jest.

A silent health to absent friends, their memories are
 bright!
A hearty health to all who keep the feast with us to-night!
A health to dear Centuria, oh, may she long abide!
A health, a health to all the world,—and the solemn ass,
 outside!

A BALLAD OF SANTA CLAUS

For the St. Nicholas Society of New York

AMONG the earliest saints of old, before the first Hegira,
I find the one whose name we hold, St. Nicholas of Myra:
The best-beloved name, I guess, in sacred nomenclature,—
The patron-saint of helpfulness, and friendship, and good-
nature.

A bishop and a preacher too, a famous theologian,
He stood against the Arian crew and fought them like a
Trojan:
But when a poor man told his need and begged an alms
in trouble,
He never asked about his creed, but quickly gave him
double.

Three pretty maidens, so they say, were longing to be
married;
But they were paupers, lack-a-day, and so the suitors
tarried.
St. Nicholas gave each maid a purse of golden ducats
chinking,
And then, for better or for worse, they wedded quick as
winking.

A BALLAD OF SANTA CLAUS

Once, as he sailed, a storm arose; wild waves the ship surrounded;
The sailors wept and tore their clothes, and shrieked "We'll all be drownded!"
St. Nicholas never turned a hair; serenely shone his halo;
He simply said a little prayer, and all the billows lay low.

The wicked keeper of an inn had three small urchins taken,
And cut them up in a pickle-bin, and salted them for bacon.
St. Nicholas came and picked them out, and put their limbs together,—
They lived, they leaped, they gave a shout, "St. Nicholas forever!"

And thus it came to pass, you know, that maids without a nickel,
And sailor-lads when tempest blow, and children in a pickle,
And every man that's fatherly, and every kindly matron,
In choosing saints would all agree to call St. Nicholas patron.

CARMINA FESTIVA

He comes again at Christmas-time and stirs us up to giving;
He rings the merry bells that chime good-will to all the living;
He blesses every friendly deed and every free donation;
He sows the secret, golden seed of love through all creation.

Our fathers drank to Santa Claus, the sixth of each December,
And still we keep his feast because his virtues we remember.
Among the saintly ranks he stood, with smiling human features,
And said, "*Be good! But not too good to love your fellow-creatures!*"

December 6, 1907.

ARS AGRICOLARIS

An Ode for the "Farmer's Dinner," University Club, New York, January 23, 1913

All hail, ye famous Farmers!
Ye vegetable-charmers,
Who know the art of making barren earth
Smile with prolific mirth
And bring forth twins or triplets at a birth!
Ye scientific fetilizers of the soil,
And horny-handed sons of toil!
To-night from all your arduous cares released,
With manly brows no longer sweat-impearled,
Ye hold your annual feast,
And like the Concord farmers long ago,
Ye meet above the "Bridge" below,
And draw the cork heard round the world!

What memories are yours! What tales
Of triumph have your tongues rehearsed,
Telling how ye have won your first
Potatoes from the stubborn mead,
(Almost as many as ye sowed for seed!)
And how the luscious cabbages and kails
Have bloomed before you in their bed
At seven dollars a head!
And how your onions took a prize

For bringing tears into the eyes
Of a hard-hearted cook! And how ye slew
The Dragon Cut-worm at a stroke!
And how ye broke,
Routed, and put to flight the horrid crew
Of vile potato-bugs and Hessian flies!
And how ye did not quail
Before th' invading armies of San José Scale,
But met them bravely with your little pail
Of poison, which ye put upon each tail
O' the dreadful beasts and made their courage fail!
And how ye did acquit yourselves like men
In fields of agricultural strife, and then,
Like generous warriors, sat you down at ease
And gently to your gardener said, "Let us have *Pease!*"

But *were* there Pease? Ah, no, dear Farmers, no!
The course of Nature is not ordered so.
For when we want a vegetable most,
She holds it back;
And when we boast
To our week-endly friends
Of what we'll give them on our farm, alack,
Those things the old dam, Nature, never sends.

ARS AGRICOLARIS

O Pease in bottles, Sparrow-grass in jars,
How often have ye saved from scars
Of shame, and deep embarrassment,
The disingenuous farmer-gent,
    To whom some wondering guest has cried,
    "How *do* you raise such Pease and Sparrow-grass?"
    Whereat the farmer-gent has not denied
    The compliment, but smiling has replied,
    "To raise such things you must have lots of glass."

From wiles like these, true Farmers, hold aloof;
Accept no praise unless you have the proof.
If niggard Nature should withhold the green
And sugary Pea, welcome the humble Bean.
Even the easy Radish, and the Beet,
If grown by your own toil are extra sweet.
Let malefactors of great wealth and banker-felons
Rejoice in foreign artichokes, imported melons;
But you, my Farmers, at your frugal board
Spread forth the fare your Sabine Farms afford.
Say to Mæcenas, when he is your guest,
"No peaches! try this turnip, 'tis my best."
Thus shall ye learn from labors in the field
What honesty a farmer's life may yield,
And like G. Washington in early youth,
Though cherries fail, produce a crop of truth

But think me not too strict, O followers of the plough;
Some place for fiction in your lives I would allow.
In January when the world is drear,
And bills come in, and no results appear,
    And snow-storms veil the skies,
    And ice the streamlet clogs,
Then may you warm your heart with pleasant lies
And revel in the seedsmen's catalogues!
What visions and what dreams are these
      Of cauliflower obese,—
Of giant celery, taller than a mast,—
      Of strawberries
Like red pincushions, round and vast,—
    Of succulent and spicy gumbo,—
    Of cantaloupes, as big as Jumbo,—
    Of high-strung beans without the strings,—
And of a host of other wild, romantic things!

    Why, then, should Doctor Starr declare
That modern habits mental force impair?
    And why should H. Marquand complain
That jokes as good as his will never come again?
    And why should Bridges wear a gloomy mien
About the lack of fiction for his Magazine?
    The seedsman's catalogue is all we need
        To stir our dull imaginations
          To new creations,
        And lead us, by the hand
        Of Hope, into a fairy-land.

ARS AGRICOLARIS

So dream, my friendly Farmers, as you will;
And let your fancy all your garners fill
With wondrous crops; but always recollect
That Nature gives us less than we expect.
Scorn not the city where you earn the wealth
That, spent upon your farms, renews your health;
And tell your wife, whene'er the bills have shocked her,
"A country-place is cheaper than a doctor."
May roses bloom for you, and may you find
Your richest harvest in a tranquil mind.

ANGLER'S FIRESIDE SONG

Oh, the angler's path is a very merry way,
  And his road through the world is bright;
For he lives with the laughing stream all day,
  And he lies by the fire at night.

    Sing hey nonny, ho nonny
    And likewise well-a-day!
    The angler's life is a very jolly life
    And that's what the anglers say!

Oh, the angler plays for the pleasure of the game,
  And his creel may be full or light,
But the tale that he tells will be just the same
  When he lies by the fire at night.

    Sing hey nonny, ho nonny
    And likewise well-a-day!
    We love the fire and the music of the lyre,
    And that's what the anglers say!

To the San Francisco Fly-Casting Club, April, 1913.

HOW SPRING COMES TO SHASTA JIM

I NEVER seen no "red gods"; I dunno wot's a "lure";
But if it's sumpin' takin', then Spring has got it sure;
An' it doesn't need no Kiplins, ner yet no London Jacks,
To make up guff about it, w'ile settin' in their shacks.

It's sumpin' very simple 'at happens in the Spring,
But it changes all the lookin's of every blessed thing;
The buddin' woods look bigger, the mounting twice as
high,
But the house looks kindo smaller, tho I couldn't tell ye
why.

It's cur'ous wot a show-down the month of April makes,
Between the reely livin', an' the things 'at's only fakes!
Machines an' barns an' buildin's, they never give no sign;
But the livin' things look lively w'en Spring is on the line.

She doesn't come too suddin, ner she doesn't come too
slow;
Her gaits is some cayprishus, an' the next ye never
know,—
A single-foot o' sunshine, a buck o' snow er hail,—
But don't be disapp'inted, fer Spring ain't goin' ter fail.

CARMINA FESTIVA

She's loopin' down the hillside,—the driffs is fadin' out.
She's runnin' down the river,—d'ye see them risin' trout?
She's loafin' down the canyon,—the squaw-bed's growin' blue,
An' the teeny Johnny-jump-ups is jest a-peekin' thru.

A thousan' miles o' pine-trees, with Douglas firs between,
Is waitin' fer her fingers to freshen up their green;
With little tips o' brightness the firs 'ill sparkle thick,
An' every yaller pine-tree, a giant candle-stick!

The underbrush is risin' an' spreadin' all around,
Jest like a mist o' greenness 'at hangs above the ground;
A million manzanitas 'ill soon be full o' pink;
So saddle up, my sonny,—it's time to ride, I think!

We'll ford er swim the river, becos there ain't no bridge;
We'll foot the gulches careful, an' lope along the ridge;
We'll take the trail to Nowhere, an' travel till we tire,
An' camp beneath a pine-tree, an' sleep beside the fire.

We'll see the blue-quail chickens, an' hear 'em pipin' clear;
An' p'raps we'll sight a brown-bear, er else a bunch o' deer;
But nary a heathen goddess or god 'ill meet our eyes;
For why? There isn't any! They're jest a pack o' lies!

HOW SPRING COMES TO SHASTA JIM

Oh, wot's the use o' "red gods," an' "Pan," an' all that
stuff?
The natcheral facts o' Springtime is wonderful enuff!
An' if there's Someone made 'em, I guess He understood,
To be alive in Springtime would make a man feel good.

California, 1913.

A BUNCH OF TROUT-FLIES

For Archie Rutledge

HERE'S a half-a-dozen flies,
Just about the proper size
For the trout of Dickey's Run,—
Luck go with them every one!

Dainty little feathered beauties,
Listen now, and learn your duties:
Not to tangle in the box;
Not to catch on logs or rocks,
Boughs that wave or weeds that float,
Nor in the angler's "pants" or coat!
Not to lure the glutton frog
From his banquet in the bog;
Nor the lazy chub to fool,
Splashing idly round the pool;
Nor the sullen hornèd pout
From the mud to hustle out!

A BUNCH OF TROUT-FLIES

None of this vulgarian crew,
Dainty flies, is game for you.
Darting swiftly through the air
Guided by the angler's care,
Light upon the flowing stream
Like a wingèd fairy dream;
Float upon the water dancing,
Through the lights and shadows glancing,
Till the rippling current brings you,
And with quiet motion swings you,
Where a speckled beauty lies
Watching you with hungry eyes.

Here's your game and here's your prize!
Hover near him, lure him, tease him,
Do your very best to please him,
Dancing on the water foamy,
Like the frail and fair Salome,
Till the monarch yields at last;
Rises, and you have him fast!
Then remember well your duty,—
Do not lose, but land, your booty;
For the finest fish of all is
Salvelinus Fontinalis.

CARMINA FESTIVA

So, you plumed illusions, go,
Let my comrade Archie know
Every day he goes a-fishing
I'll be with him in well-wishing.
Most of all when lunch is laid
In the dappled orchard shade,
With Will, Corinne, and Dixie too,
Sitting as we used to do
Round the white cloth on the grass
While the lazy hours pass,
And the brook's contented tune
Lulls the sleepy afternoon,—
Then's the time my heart will be
With that pleasant company!

June 17, 1913.

INDEX OF FIRST LINES

INDEX OF FIRST LINES

INDEX OF FIRST LINES

INDEX OF FIRST LINES

INDEX OF FIRST LINES

INDEX OF FIRST LINES

Printed in the United Kingdom
by Lightning Source UK Ltd.
129543UK00001B/183/A

9 781434 489975